IN YOUR COURT

AMANDA CIRILLI

Paperback ISBN: 979-8-9997458-4-2

eBook ISBN: 979-8-9997458-2-8

LCCN: 2026906041

Cover Design: AC Designs, J. Bosma

Editing: Kriti Tripathi of StoryArk Editing

Paper Book Formatting: AC Designs

Digital Book Formatting: Atticus

Cover Character Art: sleepingfoxy

Contents

TRIGGER WARNINGS

Please be advised that this book contains the following:
language, bullying, explicit sexual content, health scares including but not limited to fainting, anxiety, panic attacks, heart problems, and mention of near-death experiences.
This book is recommended for ages 18+.

DEDICATION

This book is dedicated to the Purdue University Men's Basketball team.
Boiler Up, Bitches!

CHAPTER 1

Holly

THE NEST CAFE IS quiet tonight, the scent of espresso and stale coffee lingering in the air. I re-read the last paragraph of my essay, sipping a lukewarm caramel latte. The usual indie playlist I enjoy isn't playing. Instead, the sports broadcaster drones through the speakers, recapping last night's basketball game.

"...and in case you missed it, the Westbridge State Hawks pulled off another big win against the Northbrooke Panthers. Star center Hunter Jace led the team with twenty-four points and thirteen rebounds, keeping the Hawks' hope alive for a March Madness spot..."

I groan. Basketball. Again.

The campus has been ablaze with excitement over Westbridge becoming genuine NCAA contenders this year, all thanks to the infamous senior center, Hunter Jace.

Everywhere on campus, people wear navy-and-gold jerseys like a second skin. The school has draped buildings and lampposts in navy-and-gold banners splashed with players' faces—mostly Hunter Jace. There is no escaping the basketball obsession. Or the extremely good-looking, charismatic, senior player at the center of it.

Not that I have anything against him personally. I just don't understand the hype. The frenzy swallowing campus feels overwhelming. Home games at Hawks Arena are sold out weeks in advance, and loud tailgates pack the campus every game weekend. It's a whole different world from mine. One where I spend most nights working at Hawthorne Library, writing essays for my lit classes or burying my nose in a book.

"...and with March Madness approaching and regional tournaments underway, all eyes are on Jace and the Hawks..."

I shrug and snap my laptop shut. "Not my eyes," I mutter under my breath as I finish my latte and pack my bag for my evening shift. Tonight, I work eight to twelve. I don't mind the late nights. I'm more of a night owl anyway. That said, the only reason students come into the library at night is for... *other* reasons. Little trysts in the stacks. I've lost count of how many times I've had to awkwardly interrupt them, only slightly jealous of the intimacy.

I've read plenty of romance novels about secret seductions in libraries after dark, but I've never experienced anything like that myself. I'm not very good at relationships, especially romantic ones. I struggle with interpersonal relationships as it is, and no one has ever expressed interest in me that way.

I'm not someone people notice. I blend into the background, just another average twenty-one-year-old. Nothing about me—or my life—is exciting. My friend group is small, consisting of one or two acquaintances more than actual friends. I don't really have hobbies outside of reading. Even my family tends to leave me alone. It's not that they don't love me. They're just not vocal about it. We were never the huggy, lovey type. More the "you did good" with a quick pat on the back. As a result, I've grown into a shy, quiet, introverted person.

As I step into the cold North Carolina evening, I tighten my jacket and grip the strap of my satchel. Hawthorne Library isn't far from the Nest, which sits at the end of Bridge Street with the other off-campus spots. It's about a ten-minute walk, depending on my pace. Westbridge State's campus is walkable and easy to navigate, especially since it isn't a large school. About fifteen thousand students attend altogether.

It's a lush campus filled with old oak trees and sweeping greenery, though in February everything lies dormant. Spring hasn't quite pushed through yet. It's trying, though. Hints of green peek through the brown. The shift from winter to spring seems slow at first, until suddenly everything bursts alive with color and the air fills with floral fragrance.

The evening air is chilly as I cross Bridge Street and step onto Westbridge campus. I follow the sidewalk into the heart of it—the Quad, the wide stretch of green where students lounge on the grass during warm spring afternoons or run through Founder's Fountain in the summer sitting at the center of the Quad.

All the paths branching through the Quad lead to academic buildings and dorms. Thankfully, my dorm sits toward the front of the campus, and Hawthorne Library is only a five-minute walk from there. The sports complexes, on the other hand, occupy the northern edge of the campus, along with Greek Row.

As I cut across the Quad, I rummage through my bag for my ID badge. It's not in its usual pocket. I frown, digging through every zipper and compartment, fingers grasping on loose papers filled with random hand-written essay ideas. Don't ask me why I don't use a spiral notebook. Something about loose-leaf paper feels right. But as the stack in my hands grows messier, so does my frustration.

"Where is that dang thing?" I mumble and walk straight into a solid wall of muscle. The impact knocks me backward. Papers slip from my grasp and fly across the sidewalk. Breath short, I shove my round metal glasses up my nose as my heart stutters in my chest.

"Whoa—sorry," a deep, warm voice says, steadying me by my elbows.

I look up.

And up.

And up.

Dark brown eyes flecked with caramel meet mine. I know who it is immediately—even without ever being this close to him before. His height alone gives him away.

A large hand wraps around my arm. It probably could twice over.

Hunter Jace.

For a heartbeat, neither of us moves. Too stunned by the collision. Up close, he isn't just the polished highlight reel television and radios stations make him out to be. There's tension in his broad shoulders. A faint crease between his brows. Someone so untouchable, suddenly looks almost... lost.

"Are you okay?" he asks, voice low, a little hoarse.

I nod, too stunned to speak.

Once I'm steady, Hunter notices the papers scattered at our feet. He crouches to gather them and hands them back to me, pausing at eye level. Another beat of silence stretches between us.

"Sorry about that. These yours?"

I stare at his hand, trying to snap myself out of his orbit.

"Uh, yeah, sorry." I take the papers quickly, our fingers brushing before I tuck them back into my bag. Why do I feel like I'm holding my breath? He drags a hand through his dark black hair, like he's done it a few times already in frustration. Even slightly disheveled, he's unfairly charming, offering me an awkward smirk.

"Hunter!" Someone calls from across the Quad, pulling our attention toward the sound. "Meeting at Whitmore House. You coming or what?"

"Yeah, yeah. I'm coming." He glances at me again, his gaze sweeping over me before settling on my eyes again. "Sorry, I gotta go."

And then he's gone, disappearing into the cool night. The sound of his footsteps fades into the distance.

I stand there a moment longer, my heart slowly settling back into rhythm. I clutch my bag closer and head toward Hawthorne Library. Of course he's in a fraternity. Whitmore House is one of the biggest on Greek Row.

I replay the collision in my mind, unsure why a ping of anxiety lingers beneath my ribs. It was just an accident. A fleeting moment. Nothing worth obsessing over. I'm a forgettable face. Unlike Hunter.

Taking a steady breath, I continue toward the library. Yet, something about his expression sticks with me.

"I don't even like basketball." I mutter. Shrugging, I walk up the sidewalk heading inside, ready for my shift.

CHAPTER 2

Holly

By Friday afternoon, I've almost convinced myself the collision with Hunter Jace had been nothing more than a weird blip in the cosmos. *Almost*. If it weren't for the fact that I keep noticing him everywhere. It's really starting to annoy me.

Walking across the Quad to my American Lit class? Hunter's there, surrounded by groupies—mostly blonde beauties hanging onto him. Grabbing a quick caramel latte at the Nest? Hunter just happens to be heading into Ballerz, the sports bar on Bridge Street. Heading back to my dorm after British Literary Concepts? Here comes Hunter, stepping out of Crestfield Science Center. It's maddening, and I don't understand why. There's no reason for me to be interested at all.

I've managed to avoid him for the past two and half years, and now, all of the sudden, the infamous Westbridge Hawks center is everywhere. Taking a deep breath, I push open the heavy oak doors of the library and head toward the back office to check in for my shift. The library is already quiet. It's Friday—so I have a feeling the night will be slow. Not that I mind. It means I'll have time to work on my current Brit Lit Concepts essay: Women's Agency in Jane Austen's *Pride and Prejudice*. I've always loved the romanticism in Austen's writing, so getting to analyze her work makes me a little giddy.

As I step into the back office, I notice a highlighter-yellow paper posted on the wall, bold lettering practically shouting at me.

ATTENTION

Mandatory Academic Help Program for Spring Athletes

Volunteer tutors needed.

Assignments begin **IMMEDIATELY** for current staff.

Please see Library Director for placements.

I stop in my tracks. Crap. This is the last thing I want to do—tutor a freshman football player on whether to use an em dash. A sigh escapes me. I'm sure it'll be fine… it's just that my schedule is already hectic this spring. Too many books to read for class. Too many analyses and papers to write. Hopefully, the tutoring won't be too time-consuming.

As I scan my ID to check in for my afternoon shift, I spot Linda Dennings, the Library Director, stepping out of the back office.

"Holly!" she calls cheerfully. "Good to see you. Come into my office for a moment, will you?"

Director Dennings is in her late fifties, with graying brown hair and crow's-feet tucked behind cat-eye spectacles. She always wears a cardigan, no matter the weather, and her hair is styled in the same French twist every day. She's thin, neatly dressed in a sheath dress, and matching heels. A string of pearls adorns her neck, with complementary pearl earrings.

Despite running Hawthorne Library, Director Dennings is warm and unapologetically extroverted. I sometimes hope to be like her when I'm older. Although, I know that my introverted personality will most likely remain unchanged.

I nod, and she leads me toward her private office, which is meticulously tidy. Dark, ornate bookcases line the back wall, filled with books and awards. I take it all in before settling down into the chair across from her desk.

"I hope you saw the notice about athlete tutoring?" Director Dennings asks.

"I just saw it, yeah."

She gives me a quick smile before waking her computer and pulling up a file. "I wanted to let you know your assignment and tutoring times. Sessions begin next week."

"Of course," I reply as evenly as possible. I can't stop my foot from tapping as I watch her click and type in the quiet office.

"Alright," she says. "So, I need to tell you that you must be discreet about your athlete. It is confidential, but I assured them you're one of our best and will maintain discretion."

My stomach tightens. Curiosity piques.

"Okay," I drawl.

After a few more clicks, Director Dennings turns back to me.

"Your tutoring sessions will be Tuesdays and Thursdays from one to two here in Hawthorne. Room E."

I pull out my planner and jot down the details. Room E is tucked in the stacks—private, away from the main area. Whoever I'm tutoring won't attract attention there. The time slot is decent, too. Between one and two, most students are in class and campus is relatively quiet. When they plan these sessions, they consider both the athlete's and the tutor's academic and extracurricular commitments. That's how they pair us—if schedules align.

"Your subject will be Shakespearean Literature," she continues, "and your athlete is Hunter Jace."

My pen wobbles in my hand, nearly slipping from my fingers.

"I'm sorry," I say, my voice thin. "Did you say Hunter Jace?"

"I did." Director Dennings replies. "You get to tutor a local celebrity. Which is exactly why we need your utmost discretion."

I take a steady breath, calming my nerves before responding. "Yes, of course. I understand. Shakespeare. Tuesdays and Thursdays... Hunter Jace. Anything else I should know?"

She shakes her head. "No, that's it. If you have questions, you'll let me know?"

"Sure," I say, rising from my seat. "Thank you."

I leave her office with my heart racing.

Hunter. Freaking. Jace. *Again*.

Why are our paths suddenly crossing like pumpkin spice in the fall? Lost in thought, I head to the reception desk and take a seat. There's a laundry list of book filings and requests waiting to be handled. Brandy—my co-worker and only real friend, a fellow junior in the Literary Studies—walks up with a cart stacked with returns. She has long sandy-blonde hair and pale blue eyes. I'm mildly envious of her curvier figure, especially since I'm so petite. Her round face and freckled button nose make her effortlessly cute.

"Hey, Holly. How's it going?" she asks cheerfully as she settles beside me, parking the cart nearby.

"Okay, I guess. Director Dennings just gave me my tutoring assignment."

"And?" Brandy quirks a brow.

I shrug. "I'm not at liberty to say."

She chuckles and shakes her head. "Of course. I got some junior baseball jock. We'll see how it goes. Apparently, he needs help with classic American literature."

"Lucky," I say with a soft laugh. "Mine needs help with Shakespeare. And honestly... who doesn't?"

"Ooh," Brandy groans. "Right? Shakespeare is complex."

Thankfully, I love British Literature. It's one of my favorite areas to study, so tutoring Hunter shouldn't be too difficult. He probably just needs to know that Romeo and Juliet both die in the end. Spoiler alert.

I can't picture him taking an advanced Shakespeare course. Maybe it's just an intro class. I took it freshman year, and it wasn't too overwhelming. I guess I'll find out Tuesday.

"Well, I've got about fifteen more minutes before I'm done for the day. Want the list for this shift?" Brandy asks. The "list" is what we call our daily tasks. Before we trade shifts, we always give the next person a quick rundown—what still needs to be done and anything unusual that happened during the day. I pull out my notebook and turn back to her.

"Sure. Lay it on me."

CHAPTER 3

Hunter

MORNING WORKOUT IS JUST wrapping up when my phone buzzes with an email notification. Usually, I ignore them. I get dozens. Other colleges trying to recruit me into their graduate programs to continue playing, NBA scouts reaching out, and recently even ESPN reporters asking for virtual interviews or short magazine features. The constant ping has started to feel like background noise. Still, it's becoming... a lot.

The past two years have been a whirlwind, especially since I helped put Westbridge State's basketball program on the map. Although I grew up close to Westbridge, they didn't recruit me. I walked on. It wasn't until I started playing that they realized what I could do. Being six-foot-nine with a seven-foot wingspan makes basketball a simple choice for me. I've always loved the game. Lived and breathed it growing up. And when I hit a major growth spurt freshman year of high school, boy did it solidify my calling.

Since then, I've followed a strict regimen to stay healthy. Morning workouts. Proper nutrition. Cool-downs. Afternoon lifts. Private coaching. Group trainings. Recreational leagues. Then varsity junior year.

Once I made varsity, I pushed everything harder—too hard. I didn't realize how far I'd taken it until I woke up in a hospital bed with my parents crying beside me. That was my wake-up call.

My heart couldn't handle the strain I was putting on it. The diagnosis isn't curable, but it's manageable. Since then, my health has had to come first.

Energy drinks and crash diets were out. Water and protein became non-negotiable. Slowly, I worked my way back to a level the doctors were comfortable clearing. It's part of why my high school stats weren't impressive. Part of why bigger programs didn't pursue me.

But, it all worked out in the end. I'm happy here at Westbridge State. And I've made my mark here. A lot of that means staying disciplined with my health. I have to monitor everything—my body, what I eat, how I recover—so I don't end up in the hospital again, shocking my heart to an unstable level.

No one knows about my condition. I haven't told a single person. The goal has always been to function like nothing's wrong. So far, I've managed it.

I drop onto the weight bench, catching my breath after the last set, music humming through my earphones. Reluctant and tired, I check my phone and open the email notification.

URGENT: Academic Standing Review

I stare at the subject for a full minute. My pulse spikes. Shit. Is this about my lit class? I knew I shouldn't have assumed it would be easy. With a shaky breath, I open the email and read it once... then again, just to make sure.

Hunter,
Your current grade in ENGL 422: The Works of William Shakespeare is below eligibility requirements for athletic participation and graduation.
Please report to my office in Alden Hall at 6:00 PM to discuss your options.
Failure to comply may result in loss of eligibility for March athletic competition should the team qualify.
Eric Lawson, M.Ed.
Senior Academic Adviser
Westbridge State University
College of Liberal Arts

I stop breathing.

Shit.

This is not good.

My entire body sinks as I exhale. March Madness—gone? Graduation—gone? I knew I wasn't doing great, but I thought I was at least passing. Even if was by the skin of my teeth. I can't let this happen. Too many people are counting on me, relying on me.

A wave of nausea rolls through me as I reread the email for the third time. Six o'clock cuts it close to the Beta Rho Chi meeting tonight, but hopefully I can get out early and still make it. Duke and UNC are playing tonight. If we make March, we could face one of them. I want to watch the game. Study the competition. Control what I can.

I take a huge gulp of my protein shake, grab my towel, and head toward the sauna. My cool-down routine after morning workouts is one of the few times I can truly relax. Twenty minutes of heat. Sweat out the stress. Quiet my head.

In the locker room, I strip out of my shirt and shorts, wrap a towel around my waist, and step inside the sauna. Twenty minutes. Just to sit and close my eyes. To just be.

"...we've already signed you up for the athlete tutoring program." Mr. Lawson explains as I sit in his office, my foot tapping uncontrollably. I've been here over an hour. He wanted to talk basketball before getting to the actual reason for the meeting. I didn't mind shooting the shit, but tonight was supposed to be mine. It was my night off, and I'd rather spend it doing what I want than sitting here.

"They've confirmed your tutoring times. Tuesdays and Thursdays from one to two in Hawthorne Library, Room E. Your tutor's name is Holly Lange."

"Okay." The name doesn't ring a bell. I'm better with faces anyway. "Sounds simple enough."

"It will be. Just show up and put in the work. Get your grade up to a sixty-eight, and you'll be fine. I know you can do it, Hunter. You're a smart kid."

"Sounds good," I push to my feet. The chair across from him is too small for me, and I've been crammed into it long enough. "Thanks for meeting with me." I extend my arm to shake his hand.

"Of course. We need our star athlete!"

He flashes a cheesy grin. I duck under the doorway on my way out and check my phone.

7:25.

If I hurry, I can still make it to Whitmore for the Beta Rho meeting. I take the stairs two at a time and shove through the doors of Alden Hall.

BAM! I reach out instinctively, steadying whatever I've just collided with.

I look down and realize I've collided with a girl.

Small. Bundled in a coat. Satchel slung across her body. She looks up at me, stunned.

"Whoa, sorry."

Her gaze drifts up my frame before meeting my eyes. Behind those round, metal glasses are wide hazel-green eyes—bright, startled, almost luminous. I take a slow breath.

"Are you okay?"

Her short brown hair hit just beneath her narrow chin, and little wisps that stop right at her eyebrows. She still hasn't answered. A few papers lie scattered near our feet, so I crouch to gather them. "These yours?"

A small nod. "Uh, yeah, sorry."

Her voice is quiet, distant, but lyrical. Our fingers brush as she takes the pages back. And I feel it. A flicker. Sudden. Uninvited. Goosebumps rise along my arms. I straighten, caught off guard by how quickly the attraction hits.

"Hunter!"

Ben's voice cuts across the Quad.

"Meeting at Whitmore House. You coming or what?" He yells and laughs as he continues on his way.

"Yeah, yeah I'm coming!" I call back.

The girl blinks, like she's just snapped out of something. There's an expression on her button face that I can't quiet read. "Sorry, I gotta go."

I step away and jog toward Ben, but before I leave the Quad, I glance back.

She's still there. Then, she exhales and walks away. And for reasons I don't understand, I hope I see her again.

CHAPTER 4

Holly

TUESDAY. 12:55 PM.

I'm sitting alone in a very empty Room E in Hawthorne Library, waiting for Hunter to grace me with his presence.

I've been here for half an hour already, working on my own homework while sipping my favorite caramel latte from the Nest. My notebook's open, the laptop's ready. Nervous energy jitters through me at the thought of sitting across from Hunter Jace for an entire hour. Helping him with Shakespeare.

Deep breaths. Take deep breaths. They help. I keep telling myself as I pretend to look busy instead of sitting here like a weirdo waiting for him to show up.

Any minute now.

1:02.

1:10.

1:15.

Okay, where the hell is he? Did he get lost? Does he even know where the library is? I glare at the ticking clock on the wall, irritation creeping in. Honestly, it wouldn't surprise me if he'd never stepped foot in here before. Most student athletes seem to skate by in college.

But, he's not just wasting his time—he's wasting mine. I don't have to be here. Well, that's not entirely true. I work here and tutor assignments come with the job. They add a little extra to my paycheck, which I'm more than happy to accept.

The minutes drag. My skin feels warm, nerves tangling with annoyance. I'm just about to pack my things up when the door handle turns.

I huff.

"Sorry, I'm late. I got dogged down by—" Hunter stops mid-sentence.

A lump forms in my throat. Seeing him again sends my anxiety spiking. A thin sheet of sweat prickles at my brow.

It takes a second, but when my voice finally returns, the frustration comes with it.

"About time," I say, standing and crossing my arms. "Do me a favor and don't be late again. I don't have time to waste."

The words comes out harsher than I intend, and guilt flickers immediately. But after waiting over twenty minutes into his session, I need to set boundaries. He must know how this is going to work. He may be a campus celebrity, but the world doesn't revolve around him. Especially not *mine*.

"Right. Of course." Hunter blinks, snapping out of whatever trance he was in. "I'm so sorry. It won't happen again."

He ducks slightly to enter the room, and then closes the door behind him. He takes a seat across from me. His long legs stretch beneath the table as he pulls out a notebook and the play he's reading.

Much Ado About Nothing.

Interesting.

"So," he asks, settling in, "how does this work?"

I raise a brow. "Tutoring?"

He grins, a rueful smile. "No, I think I get the concept. I mean, for my class. For Shakespeare. How are you going to tutor me?"

My posture loosens as I sit back down, tapping my pen against my notebook while I study him. "First, you tell me what's confusing you. Then, I figure out if it's a reading thing, a meaning thing, or 'this was written five hundred years ago and makes no sense' thing." I shrug lightly. "Then we break it down. Translate it into plain English. Map out the characters. Connect the dots. Whatever helps."

I hesitate, then add, a little softer, "I can help make it less scary."

A quiet pause settles between us, and my stomach flutters with nervous energy. For a moment, I wonder if he needs more explanation. I bite my lip—a nervous habit—and just as I'm about to fill in the silence, he speaks.

"Alright."

His voice is low, rough around the edges, as he looks down at the small book in his oversized hands. The contrast is almost amusing, and I have to fight a chuckle.

"So. *Much Ado About Nothing,*" I say, leaning forward slightly. "How far are you? What are you getting from it?"

He rests his forearms on the table, a faint crease forming between his brows. "I'm about halfway through," he says. "It's actually funny. At least... if I'm reading it right. Everyone's pretending not to care. Pretending not to be hurt. Like, it's easier to joke about love than admit you want it."

I still. Watching him speak is weirdly... appealing? Something about the way his lips move is captivating. I study him as he lets out a slow breath and starts drumming his fingers against the table.

"How about the characters?" I ask. "Any stand out?"

"Beatrice and Benedick," he says without hesitation. "They act like they're above it. Like, they're too clever for love. But really? I think they're just scared of getting hurt."

My brows lift despite myself. Maybe he isn't just all muscle. Perhaps there's a brain in there. He actually understands it better than he thinks.

"I don't know," he sighs. "Benedick talks a big game, but he's loyal. When it matters, he listens. I respect that."

"Huh," I mumble, tapping my pen against my notebook. "So what about the text speaks to you?

The sarcasm? The fear of emotional vulnerability? Maybe you're waiting for someone to trick you into falling in love."

I laugh at my own joke. Hunter doesn't. He stares at me like I've grown a second head.

Heat crawls into my cheeks. I sink slightly in my seat, suddenly very aware of the warm air in the room.

I clear my throat and glance down at the doodles in my notebook. "Obviously, I didn't mean it like you need to be tricked into loving someone. I mean, you have... options. I'm sure girls would kill each other to love you."

Why am I still talking?

I wave my hand in a vague attempt to undo the damage. "It was just a Shakespeare joke. A bad one. Um... sorry."

I resist the urge to physically facepalm. What the hell is wrong with me? Mentally, I chastise myself when I peek up at him through my glasses. He's still watching me, unreadable.

Hunter leans back in his chair. The fabric of his shirt pulls tight across his chest, and his lips twitch like he's fighting a smile. His eyes pierce mine.

"Did you just say girls would kill to love me?" His voice is low. Amused.

My face heats all over again.

"I was speaking hypothetically," I mutter. "Not that they'd actually commit murder for a chance to love you."

Smooth, Holly. Real smooth.

Hunter chuckles, then shrugs. "Hypothetical or not, that kind of made my day."

He studies me for a beat. "You're the girl I bumped into last week."

My brain short-circuits. "What?"

"Yeah," he nods, rubbing his smooth jawline with his thumb. "I remember. My distraction, your apparent existential crisis, and *bam*. We collided."

I bury my face in my hands. "Oh my God. I was hoping you'd forgotten."

He laughs, leaning forward again, elbows resting on the table. "I recognized you the moment I walked in. I'm glad you're okay."

I give a tight, mock laugh. "I'm fine. Just a little mortified. It wasn't my finest hour." I clear my throat and meet his eyes again. A beat lingers between us. "We should probably stick to the task at hand?"

We hold each other's gaze a second too long before he relents. "Alright, fine. *Much Ado* it is."

"Good." I sigh. "So, do you have an assignment you need help with?"

I drag my notebook closer just as he slides a question sheet across the dark wooden table.

"Okay," I read aloud. "Question one. How do Beatrice and Benedick's first interactions reveal their relationship dynamic? What literary devices does Shakespeare use to portray their feelings?" I glance up at Hunter. He's intently staring at me. "Any thoughts?"

He shrugs. "I guess... they're kind of mean to each other. Like, aggressively so. Feels like unresolved anger issues."

A snort escapes my mouth before I can stop it. "Not technically wrong. Maybe don't phrase it like that on your paper."

He grins—a pretty boy smile. One that surely makes girl's panties wet.

Oh, why did my mind go there? My mouth suddenly feels dry and I swallow.

Unbothered, he shrugs. "Fine. How about this—they insult each other so much that it's basically flirting. You know how people say, when a guy and girl tease each other, it means they secretly like each other? Same thing here. Old-school roasting equals flirting. Shakespeare just fluffs it up in fancy English."

I raise a brow. "Okay. That's actually closer to one of the literary devices you can highlight. It's called 'wit'. Quick, clever exchanges that prove they're equals. Neither one wants to lose, so they hide behind jokes and jabs."

"Like deflecting?" he asks, tapping his pencil against the page. "If they're busy arguing, they don't have to admit they're into each other."

I point my pen at him. "Exactly. Classic emotional repression."

"Huh." He scribbles something down before looking up again. "So. Literary devices. What else?"

I gather my thoughts. "You could mention verbal irony, saying the opposite of what they mean. Wordplay. Metaphor."

"Got it." He writes again, and then his warm brown eyes meet mine. As I study them, I can see little flecks of caramel threaded into them.

"Let me see what you've got for question one." I say, gesturing toward his notebook. He turns it around.

Beatrice and Benedick pretend to hate each other, but their insults are a way of avoiding how they really feel. Shakespeare uses sarcasm, wordplay, and irony to show their arguments are just emotional armor. They're scared to be honest, so they flirt by fighting.

I read it twice, expecting to find something to correct. But it's actually solid. Clear. Insightful. To the point.

"Okay," I say slowly. "Yeah, Hunter. That's actually good."

He flashes me a grin. "So, passable good? Or 'I'd give you an A' good?"

I roll my eyes, and chuckle. "It's not perfect thesis-level good. But I'd say a solid B-plus, in my opinion."

I refuse to inflate his ego any more than necessary. He can't be dominant on the court *and* good at Shakespeare. That's against jock-athlete mentality, right?

Hunter leans back in his chair and drags his unusually long fingers through his short black hair, leaving it slightly mussed. "I'll take it," he happily states as if a weight just lifted off his shoulders.

I laugh, feeling some of my nerves loosen. "You're such a jock."

"A jock who's starting to understand Shakespeare," he counters. "Admit it. You're a little impressed." He winks at me.

Freaking. Winks! If my panties weren't wet before from all those boyish grins, then they might be now.

I clear my throat and shove his notebook back across the table. "Okay, Shakespeare. Let's get to question two before your ego needs its own chair."

Hunter laughs—full and unrestrained—and for the first time since he walked in, the room feels easy.

CHAPTER 5

Holly

I'M SITTING CROSS-LEGGED ON my bed in my dorm room at Meadowbrooke Commons, happily re-reading *Persuasion* by Jane Austen. It's one of my favorites. It's one of those rare quiet night ins, no library shift, no urgent homework. Just me and Austen.

My dorm room isn't big. It's more like a closet, especially since it's a single and not a double like most of the rooms in Meadowbrooke. Most upperclassmen move off-campus, but that never made sense for me. I don't have a car, I work odd hours at the library, and I don't exactly have a group of friends to split rent with. So here I am.

Meadowbrooke is one of the nicer dorms anyway. It's close to Bridge Street, just off the Quad, and only a five-minute walk to Hawthorne. For me, it's ideal.

The room itself is simple: a twin wooden bed, a matching desk, and a little corner I've claimed for my Keurig, snacks, and mini fridge. There's a built-in closet with four drawers that hold my modest clothing collection. Above them hangs a narrow mirror on the wall, where I could apply make-up—if I ever wore any.

It's a basic setup. Perfect for my low-maintenance life.

I've decorated the walls with a few framed prints I've hung using removable hooks. Images of rolling hills of the British countryside and dreamy photos of sprawling old libraries I'll probably never visit. A small bookshelf sits in the corner beside my Moon Pod chair, my favorite place to curl up and read.

Tonight, I decide to read in bed beneath the string of fairy lights I hung overhead. My room is a warm and inviting—a quiet haven, even if I never have guests. When I'm not in class, at work, or hiding out at the Nest, this is where I am. Home.

A cup of tea rests on my nightstand, pillows stacked behind me as I reread my favorite scene from *Persuasion*—Captain Wentworth's letter to Anne.

The ultimate feet-kicking moment. I've read it more times than I can count.

I can listen no longer in silence. I must speak to you by such means as are within my reach. You pierce my soul...

BUZZ.

My phone vibrates violently against the nightstand, ripping me out of the moment. I ignore it, assuming it's my mom doing one of her routine check-ins, and return to the page.

I am half agony, half hope... I have loved none but you...

BUZZ.

I exhale sharply. "What the heck?"

I set the book aside and grab my phone.

Hey, Short-Stack.

...Thanks for the help yesterday.

I stare at the screen; my brows knit together tightly. It's not mom. I don't recognize this number.

I think you have the wrong number, sorry.

Three dots appear almost immediately.

Wow, cold. Definitely not the wrong number, Holly.

A chill runs down my spine.

Who is this?

I chew on my lip as I wait, nerves bundling up in my stomach. The response comes quickly.

It's Hunter. Obviously.

I stare at the message and release a slow breath. Of course it's him. Only Hunter would interrupt Captain Wentworth's confession with a random nickname and a smug "obviously." I update the contact from "Unknown" to "Hunter".

You could've led with that. Honestly, how'd you get my number, anyway?

Hello? Tutor Program…

Of course. I roll my eyes. Tutors usually exchange numbers with their athletes for road games and emergencies. I forgot to get his yesterday. Apparently, he didn't forget mine. Somehow...No problem.

Besides, where's the suspense in saying "Hey, it's that basketball player you're tutoring". Mystery is more fun.

I roll my eyes, again. This guy...

I don't think you realize how mildly terrifying "mystery" can be for a young woman. Besides, where did "short-stack" come from? What does that mean?

You're like a whole 5'2…Seemed fitting.

I almost growl at my phone, typing furiously.

Excuse me! I'm a "*whole*" 5'5!!

Still a short-stack.

I narrow my eyes.

I'm blocking you.

Whoa, whoa, whoa, calm down, stacks. I'm just teasing you. Besides, I get made fun of for my height all the time.

A reluctant smile tugs at my mouth. Of course he gets teased for his height. He's ginormous. A walking skyscraper.

Anyway, you watching the game tonight?

Why would I do that?

Ouch…To support your favorite pupil, of course.

Right, of course. No. Wasn't planning on it. I have a date with Austen.

The three little dots appear. Disappear, and then reappear. He's thinking.

…Who is Austen? And do I know him?

I laugh out loud—soft and surprised. The kind that bubbles up before I can stop it. The kind you don't expect from a text conversation. Especially not one involving a six-foot-nine headache of a star athlete.

Tall, dark, and fictional. You wouldn't stand a chance.

I've got the tall and dark part…

I pause. Is he… flirting?

A smirk curves my lips as I reread the message. Little butterflies swarm in my stomach. Another text pops up before I can reply.

…so I don't know him?

No, Hunter. Austen is an author. As in Jane Austen…actual emotional depth.

Oh. So…you're reading?

Very good.

I can't help myself from teasing him.

So…no plans?

I stare at the screen, amused. I can practically hear the smugness in his tone. I start typing something clever, then delete it. Three little dots appear again. And this time, they linger.

You should come to Hawks Arena. Tip-off's at 7:45. I'll even read your book to you afterwards if that's what it takes.

I roll my eyes—hard. I've probably exercised those eye muscles more in the past fifteen minutes than in the past three years. And yet, a tiny traitorous part of me smiles. The banter is a little endearing. Am I flattered? No. Yes. Maybe. My feelings are mixed, but there's a light, giddy hum beneath it all.

Goodnight, Hunter.

I set my phone face-down and pick *Persuasion* back up. I read. I try to read, at least.

Time slips by and I can't help but notice.

7:40.

Five minutes before tip-off.

I have no intention of going. Crowds like that freak me out. Still, I pause, inhale, and stare at the ceiling. A sigh escapes my mouth.

Jumping off my bed, I amble to grab my laptop from the desk. I climb back under the covers, settling it on my lap.

A quick search tells me I can watch the game on ESPN+. Paid subscription.

My shoulders slump. I chew on my lower lip staring at the screen like it might decide for me. I can pay for a subscription. It's not *that* expensive; I can swing it.

I groan. *Am I really doing this?*

Apparently, yes.

I grab my wallet, pull out my credit card, and sign up for the streaming service, muttering under my breath the entire time. Hell might actually be freezing over. The game loads. The sportscasters run through pre-game analysis as the camera sweeps across the court, catching players focused in their warm-up.

And then—

There he is. In all his frustrating, ESPN-glorified glory. Hunter Jace. Dark hair, slightly mussed. Sweat beads along his brow as he moves through drills. He's wearing a sleeveless navy-and-gold jersey, the

Hawks mascot emblazoned across his chest, a single compression sleeve hugging his right arm. His shorts hang just right, trimmed in gold along the sides. ESPN+ does not miss.

My mouth actually falls open as I stare at the screen. How am I immediately drawn to a basketball player?

He looks… gorgeous. I don't understand it. Hunter cracks a joke to a teammate, then flashes that dangerous, boyish grin…and has the audacity to wink at the camera.

Of course he does.

The man is a walking rom-com cover. Annoyingly attractive doesn't even begin to cover it. Yet, there's something else there. Something behind that grin. A flicker I can't quiet name. For reasons I don't fully understand, I find myself caring. Which is absurd. I barely know him. We've met once… well… twice, if I count the run-in. That hardly qualifies as anything. He probably has entire fan club lined up to orbit him. And yet here I am, the quiet one, watching from my bed, heart beating a little too fast.

The game tips off, and within minutes I realize I have absolutely no idea what I'm looking at. There's a ball. There are very tall men moving at alarming speeds. The arena is a blur of shouting, chanting, and squeaking sneakers. Whistles blow every few seconds, or at least it feels that way. It's chaotic. Loud. Overstimulating. I try to follow along. I even Google a few of the terms the sportscasters throw around, but mostly it's sneakers on polished wood and someone occasionally sliding across the floor with a rag or mop of some kind.

Yuck. I would not survive that job.

Hunter is easy to spot. Not just because he's the tallest on the court, but because he moves like he owns it. He flies up and down the hardwood as if it's an extension of him. Every stride he takes is effortless. And it's... beautiful to behold. It's almost as if I'm watching an elaborate dance from the Regency era. It's his stage. And he doesn't even have to try. There's no posing. No cocky grin for the cameras. Just motion—fluid, focused, free. He isn't performing. He's playing. And somehow, that's even more captivating.

I don't realize I'm leaning forward until my laptop tilts on my lap and the stream abruptly disappears. "No!"

I scramble, reloading ESPN+. Heart thudding as the screen buffers. Fifteen seconds later it's back, and I exhale as Hunter spins, passes and cuts across the court again. The camera tracks him. The announcers call his name, talking about some season stats that I don't understand. Guess, I'll have to read up some basketball jargon. The crowd swells, loud even through laptop speakers.

It's overwhelming.

And then, a defender barrels into him.

There's a sharp collision. An elbow—maybe a shoulder—slams into Hunter's chest.

Hunter stumbles. At first, it looks like nothing. Just a misstep. But then he slows. His hand presses against his chest. Something changes in his face. Not dramatic. Not theatrical. Something wrong. As if he's wincing.

My stomach drops.

He takes one unsteady step.

And then he falls. He just... collapses.

Gasps ripple through the arena. Then, it's utter silence. One moment he's airborne. The next, his body is crumpled on the hardwood. I bolt upright, the laptop nearly sliding off my knees. I grab it just in time.

The camera cuts away too fast, following the ball like nothing happened. The announcers falter. Words trip over each other. When the camera returns, Hunter is still down. Teammates crowd around him, forming a tight circle. Trainers sprint onto the court. Then more people. Medics rush in. A growing wall of bodies.

He doesn't move.

My heart hammers within my chest and my stomach sinks. I drag the screen closer to my face without meaning to, as if proximity will give me answers.

The announcers offer nothing useful. Just speculation. Hesitation. The screen cuts to commercial.

He's just winded.

He took a hard hit.

He'll get up.

Right?

The broadcast returns. The circle has widened. There's now EMTs. And a cart. He's still on the floor.

A cold wave moves through me.

The room suddenly feels too quiet. The air's too thin.

And I can't breathe.

CHAPTER 6

Holly

I've read the same sentence four times now. Something about Shakespeare and mistaken identity. Which feels ironic, considering I'm pretending I'm not spiraling over someone who collapsed on national television and hasn't texted me back.

There's still been no real update. Just that he collapsed and he's in the hospital. That his family is requesting privacy.

My mind keeps replaying his face. The way his expression shifted right before he fell. The moment something clearly went wrong.

The tutoring room is painfully quiet. Fluorescent lights buzz faintly overhead. The clock ticks with annoying precision.

I check my phone again.

Nothing.

I sent the first text last night, hoping I'd get some response.

Are you okay?

Then another this morning.

Just checking in.

No reply. No read receipts. Just silence.

Heavy and suffocating.

He was supposed to be here ten minutes ago. But he was over twenty minutes late on Tuesday. Maybe this is just his MO. Fashionably late.

That's the optimistic version.

I ignore the steady climb of my pulse.

I flip my notebook open and force my eyes back to the words.

"Disguise is thus a kind of truth..."

Tick.

Tick.

Tick.

Damn clock. Mocking me.

1:28.

He's coming, right?

I try to steady myself. He's fine. He's okay. After the collapse, they called the game. The team looked shaken and I understand why. I'm still shaken from seeing it on screen. Westbridge had been ahead by four points—technically a win. But at what cost?

My foot taps. My pen clicks in rhythm. The room feels smaller by the second. The door opens. I look up instantly, relief flooding through me, but my smile immediately fades when I see Brandy.

She chuckles. "Nice to see you, too."

"Sorry," I say quickly. "It's not you. I'm just a little on edge."

She flicks her sandy-blonde hair over her shoulder and steps inside, her pale eyes scanning my face. "I just came to tell you the athletic office called," she says. "Hunter won't be here today. Maybe not next week either."

The words land heavy. My stomach drops. Nausea overwhelms me. "Did they say why?" I ask, too quickly. "Is he okay?" I don't know if she watched the game last night. I doubt it because I know she isn't into basketball either. But maybe the athletic office told her something.

"Nope," she crossed her arms and shrugged. "No reason. Just that he's unable to come."

Unable to come?

I inhale slowly, fighting the wave of queasiness caught in my throat. "Okay. Well, thanks for letting me know."

I start gathering my things, trying to keep my hands steady.

Brandy pauses at the door, studying me. "Sooo," she says lightly, one brow lifting, "Hunter Jace is your athlete?"

I nod, suddenly at a loss of words.

"That's cool," Brandy says.

"Well, we only had one session," I reply quickly. "And now I'm not even sure if there'll be another. So, it's not a big deal." I try to sound neutral, but it comes out strained. Brandy looks at me the way she would if a book was shelved in the wrong section.

"Are you okay? What am I missing?"

"Did you watch the game last night?" I ask, already moving toward the door. She follows.

"No. You know I don't follow basketball."

"He collapsed," I whisper as we walk through the stacks and toward the front. "On the court."

"Shit," she exhales. "Is he okay?"

"I don't know." The words tumble out before I can stop them. "One second he was sprinting, and next someone hit him and he just fell. They cut the camera away like it was nothing. I kept waiting for them to say that he got back up, that he was fine, but they didn't. He hasn't texted me back and— "

I stop myself, dragging in a breath.

"I just can't stop thinking about it..." I continue, quieter now. "There's no news. Just that he's in the hospital and his family wants privacy. I refreshed every site for hours... Nothing. The school paper just said we won, that he's hospitalized. No actual update."

I stop walking.

Brandy turns toward me, arms still crossed over her chest, her blonde-brow raised. Her freckled nose wrinkles. "So," she says carefully, "it sounds like someone caught a little more than basketball last night."

I glare at her, but she softens immediately. "Hey. I'm kidding." Her voice lowers. "Are you okay? Seeing that kind of thing is terrifying. Especially when it's someone you know. Even if it is your very tall, very hot study buddy."

I grimace and look away. "I just hate not knowing." My voice is smaller than I expect. "I hope he's okay."

Brandy walks me to the library entrance before heading back to her shift. "If I hear anything through the grapevine, I'll let you know."

"Thanks." I say, as I step out of Hawthorne.

It's midnight. I'm at my desk, supposedly working on my Women's Agency essay for Brit Lit. A cup of chamomile tea sits beside my laptop, steaming curling lazily upward-it's doing a better job relaxing than I am. The cursor blinks on my screen like it's mocking me.

Elizabeth exercises agency in subtle but meaningful ways, often pushing against the constraints of—

I pause, then delete that crap again.

This is the third time I've tried to write it.

I lean back in my chair, let out a sigh, and stare up at the string lights along my ceiling. The room is quiet, too quiet. Every sound feels amplified by what isn't there. Especially the silence from him. I haven't sent that many texts. Just a couple. Just enough to know he's okay.

There's still no update anywhere. The usual talk-of-the-town celebrity now feels like a ghost. Like he vanished. My stomach twists. Oh my God, I shouldn't have had that thought...

Nope. Absolutely not going there.

Everything is fine.

I take a sip of my tea and reach for my phone out of habit.

Nothing.

Just as I set it down, it vibrates. The screen lights up.

Hey.

Sorry I didn't text sooner.

My stomach flips as I stare at those words. A wave of relief floods my senses. My eyes sting unexpectedly.

He's okay—he's replied. Before I can even breathe properly, another message shows up.

Guess you watched the game?

I just stare at the screen. Relief is still flooding through me, but something else rises beneath it. Frustration. Hot and immediate.

Is that your way of saying "Sorry I collapsed in front of thousands of people and then ghosted you for 24 hours?"

Oof. Brutal. I did say sorry.

Barely. Two weenie texts don't count as an apology.

Okay, fine. Official apology incoming:

I, Hunter Jace, apologize for ghosting you, worrying you, scaring you, and/or making you feel feelings.

I huff.

Feelings?

I don't have feelings. None whatsoever. Right? Perhaps my anxiety is irrational. I have no business reacting like this over someone I've met twice.

I didn't feel feelings…I'm simply concerned for my pupil.

Right. Of course. Ever the studious tutor. Good to know you're passionately concerned about all your athletes.

I don't correct him. I don't tell him he's the only one. That would be way too close to admitting something.

I'll make it up to you…We good?

I hesitate. Curious what "making up to you" entails. Also aware that I need to remain impartial.

Sure. We're good. I'm just glad you're okay.

There's a brief pause before he replies.

Thanks, Short-Stack. For worrying about me.

My thumbs hover over the keyboard for a moment. I don't reply, though. Not because I don't want to. But because I don't trust what might come out if I do.

CHAPTER 7

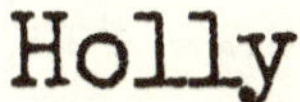

I WAKE TO A gray, chilly day on Saturday morning. I don't usually sleep in, but after this week—after everything—I needed it. I'm barely halfway out of bed, about to go to the dorm bathrooms, when my phone buzzes. I check it immediately.

> Meet me at Nook's at 10.

I read it again, just to make sure I've read it correctly.

My eyes hover to the time, and it's already 9:15.

"Shit."

I dive for my closet. Clothes fly past my hands—skirts, cardigans, oversized sweaters. Very librarian-core. Nothing cute or sporty. Nothing even remotely date-like. My throat bobs as my stomach starts churning.

Why am I thinking date-like?

It's not a date. He didn't ask me out. He just told me to meet him. At Nook's.

It's only my favorite vintage off-campus bookstore. The only place where I read apart from my dorm or the library.

How would he even know that? He wouldn't. Maybe he just wants to reschedule tutoring since he missed Thursday. That's all.

I grab a cream-colored baggy sweater with tiny embroidered flowers around the neckline and cuffs, a forest-green corduroy skirt, warm tights and my chunky Mary Jane's—something that'll hopefully help me feel not so pint-sized against his skyscraper height.

Outfit decided, I rush to the bathroom, speed through my routine, and head back to my room to get dressed.

After about twenty minutes, I step out of Meadowbrooke and I'm off to Bridge Street. The Nook sits at the very end—a tiny storefront tucked into a long stretch of brick building. I consider detouring to the Nest for a caramel latte. But Hunter's the one who set the time, and I don't want to be late. So I head straight to the Nook. Maybe after I meet up with him, I can get my latte.

I hug my coat tighter as a winter breeze cuts across the Quad. There's another game tonight, and students are already staking out tailgate spots.

I shake my head, half amused, half incredulous. Who willingly eats hot dogs and drinks beer at ten in the morning? I stifle a laugh as I continue past the Founder's Fountain, which is off today, and turn onto Bridge Street.

And I see him.

Hunter Jace stands outside the Nook, leaning against the brick, backpack slung over one shoulder. Navy Westbridge hoodie and a pair of faded jeans cling to his body unfairly well... Boy, does he look delicious.

I notice two to-go coffee cups resting in his large hands and as I get closer, I realize they're from the Nest.

"Hey," I say as I approach, trying to sound casual. Relief floods me at the sight of him standing there. Upright. Solid. Real. I scan him quick and subtle, before lifting my gaze up to his face. His eyes meet mine and he flashes a smile—that charming smile.

"Hey, Short-Stack." He hands me one of the cups. "Got your favorite."

A random urge to hug him jolts through me, but I keep my arms at my sides. I want to ask him how he's feeling, if he's okay. I want to know what happened, yet I hesitate, unsure if he's ready to talk about it. Instead, I take the cup and sip. Caramel latte.

I raise a brow. "How did you know?" I pretend to study him. "Have you been spying on me? Is this part of your charm offense?"

"I have my sources." He takes a sip from his own cup like he didn't just dodge the question.

I chuckle. "Not suspicious at all. But, thank you. I was definitely debating a stop."

"Then I saved you the trip. You're welcome."

There's a quiet beat. I stare down at the cup in my hands, suddenly fascinated by the cardboard sleeve. "So..." I shuffle my feet. "Is this a make-up tutoring session or...?"

"No." He shakes his head, and his smile softens. "It's to make up for ghosting you."

Oh.

I blink, caught off guard by the sincerity in his voice. For a split second, I forget how hands work and nearly drop the cup.

Smooth.

Flustered, I nod and look away, very invested in a tiny pebble near my shoe. He reaches for the door to the Nook and swings it open, stepping aside with an exaggerated bow.

"After you, Stacks. I believe you have a book to choose, and I have a debt to repay."

I roll my eyes, but my smile gives me away as I step past him. He holds the door, still smirking like he didn't just short circuit my brain by offering to buy me a book.

Inside, the Nook wraps around me like a warm hug. The scent of old paper and cinnamon hangs in the air. It's quiet, peaceful—just a couple of bookish people browsing the shelves. Hunter ducks, he literally ducks, to clear the doorway. He looks so out of place in my tiny corner of the world that I fight a laugh.

"Okay," he murmurs behind me, voice lowered instinctively. "Show me how this works."

"You've never been in a bookstore?" I quip, a grin tugging at my lips.

He hisses through his teeth, scrubbing a hand through his dark hair. "I've been in one. Just not voluntarily."

I blink. "That is... genuinely upsetting."

"What can I say? The library and I have an understanding. I don't bother it, it doesn't bury me in existential crisis."

I roll my eyes and head deeper into the store. Hunter follows a step behind. His lone stride equals at least five of my steps, so he's clearly trying hard not to overwhelm me. I stop between two narrow shelves and trail my fingers along the spines, pretending to consider my options—even though I know exactly where I'm going. My hand pauses on a pastel cover nestled between two brighter titles. Without thinking, I pull it free.

A contemporary rom-com. Cute, cartoon couple, title in bubbled letters, fake dating, and one bed. I flip it open, just to glance at the first line.

I don't notice him leaning in until his voice brushes my ear. "Oh wow," he murmurs. "Deep stuff."

I jump and snap the book shut. The warmth of his breath sends a shiver down my spine. "Do you mind?" I say, turning to glare at him.

He doesn't look sorry in the slightest. His deep brown eyes threaded with flecks of caramel spark with amusement. "Just appreciating your literary taste."

I clutch the book to my chest, willing my pulse to calm. "Well," I retort, "some of us enjoy stories that don't involve balls and scoreboards, Hot-Shot."

He freezes.

Then slowly, real slowly, that grin morphs into a full-on megawatt smile. His eyebrows lift like I've just handed him the winning lottery ticket. At first, I think he's about to tease me for saying "balls", but then—

"...Hot-Shot?"

Oh no.

Heat floods my face.

Oh, no no no.

Why, of all the things to let slip, did I let that nickname in my head leave my lips? I open my mouth. Close it. Even consider diving into a stack of hardcovers and living there indefinitely.

"Absolutely a figment of your inflated imagination," I mutter.

"Sure it was," he smirks, taking another sip of coffee.

I finally manage to tear my eyes away from his entirely too-pleased expression and look down at the rom-com book in my hand. I flip it over, pretending to read the blurb with intense concentration.

"So, that's the winner?" He nods toward it, smile still plastered on his face. "Is it something I could enjoy? Or strictly for banter and sexual tension?"

I chuckle, clutching the book to my chest, and start toward the register. "It's called escapism. Some of us appreciate happy endings."

He studies me a second longer than necessary. "Yeah," he says, quieter now. "I do too." The tease in his smile shifts just enough to make my heart stutter. The air between us suddenly feels hotter, the innuendo not lost on me as he dips close to my face. There's a beat—just one—but it stretches long and slow.

I bite my bottom lip, an unconscious reflex I regret the second his eyes drop. Then his thumb lifts. Gently, he pulls my lip free from my teeth. My breath catches in my throat and I swear the ground tilts. His gaze is steady, scorching, and I feel my face warming with a blush that's most likely creeping all the way down my neck.

"I'll take that."

My heart might actually stop.

Before I can fully process what just happened, his hand shifts, slow and easy, as he plucks the book from my grasp. "And this, too."

And then he turns and walks toward the checkout counter like he didn't just melt my nervous system into a puddle. I remain rooted in place. Lip tingling, panties wet, and my dignity questionable. My heart pounds so hard against my ribs I can feel it in my throat. Heat climbs up my neck and settles beneath my skin, my stomach fluttering.

Hunter pays for the book, calm as ever. I follow him out of the store in a daze. The cool air hits my face, helping steady me. I inhale slowly, trying to reclaim some composure. He hands me the paper bag.

"Thanks," I manage, still flushed.

"Of course," His voice is softer now. "Hopefully it makes up for my terrible texting etiquette."

I nod, "I think it qualifies."

There's a beat of silence before we both start to speak at the same time. Then laugh.

"You first," I blurt.

"I have one more thing for you." He swings his backpack around and unzips it. I watch, curious, still trying to come down from cloud nine, as he pulls out a folded piece of fabric.

I stare at it, puzzled.

"You should come to the game tonight."

"What?" I blink.

"I'm not playing," he says. "Coach has me benched until I'm cleared. But I've got a seat for you. VIP treatment, obviously."

Before I can form a response, he presses the navy-and-gold jersey—a Hawks jersey—in my hands.

His jersey. Name. Number. Everything.

"Figured you could wear it," he adds lightly. "You know... if you're done dating Austen."

I snort—loud and totally ungraceful. It just escapes. My brain short-circuits, but my smile softens as I look down at the fabric. I lift my gaze to his.

"Are you asking me out, Hunter?"

He shrugs like it's nothing. Like, it isn't everything.

"I'm asking you to sit courtside with popcorn and a front-row view of my best sulking," he says rummaging a hand through his hair. "But yeah. Maybe I am."

My fingers curl around the jersey. It's soft. Feels substantial. The number thirteen is embroidered across it. Thirteen. I stare at it a moment longer than necessary.

"Why thirteen?" I ask as I glance up at him.

He chuckles, embarrassed. "It's my birthday. I'm not very creative."

My head snaps up. "Really?" I ask, maybe a little too enthusiastically.

He laughs at my expression. "Yeah. That's not something I'd lie about. Why?"

I glance back at the number and then at him.

"It's mine too."

"Shit. Really?" Now he laughs harder. "Wait, what month?"

"October."

"Ah, June," he grins.

There's a quiet pause between us. Not awkward. Just... charged.

"Kind of a weird coincidence, don't you think?" He finally says. "Our birthdays fall on the thirteenth?"

"Kind of," I giggle. He's making it sound like it's destiny or something.

I stare down at the jersey in my hand, rubbing my thumb over the soft material. "This doesn't mean I'm officially a Hawks fan," I tease, lifting it slightly.

Hunter scoffs, grinning. "Wouldn't dream of asking that much commitment." He tilts his head. "So...the game tonight. Want to come?"

I hesitate holding the jersey like it might catch fire from the heat. I'm definitely pink. Then I nod. Just once. "Okay, I'll come."

His smile stretches wide—genuine, unguarded, happy—and something in my chest does an embarrassing dramatic flip.

"Hot-Shot and Short-Stack taking over the VIP section," he says. "People aren't ready."

"I know I'm not," I shoot back, though a spike of nerves flares beneath my ribs. He walks me to the corner of Bridge Street.

"See you tonight."

"Yeah," I reply. "Courtside popcorn and sulking. Can't wait." He gives me a lopsided smile, then takes a few steps backward.

"Don't be late, Short-Stack." He calls back with a full air of confidence before turning toward the Quad. I stand there a second, jersey and bookstore bag clutched to my chest, half-finished latte cooling in my other hand. I don't know what this feeling is.

But I think I want to find out.

CHAPTER 8

Holly

IF HELL WAS PAVED in navy-and-gold, it would look exactly like this. The sidewalk outside of Hawks Arena pulses with bodies. Too many bodies. People chant and yell, wave foam fingers, and blast those long plastic horns—vuvuzelas, I think—that vibrates straight through my skull. There's a swarm of Westbridge basketball jerseys around me, while others are painted in school colors. Someone's grilling sausages on a portable grill balanced far too close to the sidewalk. People are doing beer funnels and I just can't help but think: This is a basketball game?

It feels less like a sports event and more like a loud, unhinged cult.

Football, I understand. I've seen that frenzy on campus before. But basketball? I never realized how wild the fandom was. Apparently, success breeds chaos.

I tighten my grip on my messenger bag and lower my head as I shuffle through a security checkpoint. I take deep breaths as I navigate through my worst nightmare. My stomach twists with nervous energy as I pull up Hunter's earlier text.

> Name's on the list. Head to Will Call just outside the arena doors. Show your ID. See you soon, Short-Stack.

I reread it for the fifth time, like it might magically calm me. It doesn't.

The crowd thickens as I follow the signs toward Will Call. Drunk students shout over each other, laughter slurring at the edges. Someone bumps into me hard enough that I nearly lose my footing. Alarmed of avoiding that further, I make my way through the crowd, like a salmon swimming upstream. Small. Outnumbered. In danger of being trampled. For a fleeting second, I consider turning around. Going back to my quiet dorm room.

But instead, I inhale slowly and keep moving.

When I reach the Will Call booth, I nearly groan at the line. For a second, I consider pulling out a book from my bag, because yes, I brought one. Something to support me emotionally. Instead, I stare up at the electric marquee.

WESTBRIDGE HAWKS vs. FULTON TECH DYNAMOS: SOLD OUT.

Twenty minutes later, I finally reach the window and tell the lady dressed in a navy polo that I'm supposed to have tickets and give her my name. She sighs as if she's bored and asks me for an ID. She glances at the screen, and her brow raises before she reaches beneath the counter and hands me a sleek navy envelope—not a printed ticket—an envelope. Of course. I step aside and open it carefully.

VIP LOUNGE ACCESS

SECTION A1 – COURTSIDE: PLAYER BENCH ACCESS
GUEST OF #13 – HUNTER JACE.

My stomach flips. Not just because of his name printed in bold… okay, maybe a little because of that. But because this just got very real. I am so outside my comfort zone I feel like I might faint.

I take a steadying breath and step through the arena doors. The noise hits me like physical force. It's like stepping to the center of a living, breathing storm. The industrial ceiling soars above me in a domed arc of steel and lights. Massive screens flash player stats, hype reels, screaming crowd prompts. Everything moves. Everything roars.

The air smells like a county fair crashed into a gym—pretzels, popcorn, kettle corn, pizza, hot dogs, and beer. A wave of navy-and-gold surges through the concourse. Painted faces. Glittered cheeks. Costumes. Jerseys. Alumni juggling kids and souvenir cups. People are everywhere and it takes me a moment gather myself and figure out where I'm supposed to go.

Vendors shout above bass-heavy music that rattles through my bones. They're selling everything from nachos to foam fingers to sixty-dollar hoodies. One guy nearly knocks another balancing four beers. Another carries a tray of chili-cheese fries that, despite everything, look wildly appetizing. I scan the signs for section A1 while weaving through hordes of students and people munching on peanuts. I am completely, hopelessly lost.

Eventually, I spot an arena worker and decide to approach him for help.

The moment she sees my ticket, her posture shifts.

"Oh," she says, "This way."

I'm guided through a separate entrance, away from the tide of students pouring into the general seating. The hallway is quieter. Thank God.

Framed photos line the walls—championship teams, alumni who went pro. All two of them—both from the sixties.

The lighting softens as we step into a private VIP lounge. It's restrained. A buffet gleams along one wall and a bar along the other. The crowd here is small. Many of them are wearing polos, blazers, and tailored coats. Either they're the donors or well-connected alumni.

I suddenly become hyper-aware of my outfit.

The Hunter Jace #13 jersey.

I have a long-sleeved shirt beneath it and a pair of high-waisted, straight jeans with white Keds on my feet. I feel so out of place among the fancy folk.

A waiter approaches. "Beverage?"

"Water," I say quickly. He returns with a bottle of Fiji water which feels unnecessarily fancy. I take it and move toward a set of double doors at the far end of the lounge. I push them open. And everything explodes.

The arena unfolds in a massive wide oval, lights blazing, sound crashing down in waves. I'm literally on the floor and thousands of bodies rise around me in a vertical wall of noise. I think I read somewhere that this arena can hold about twelve thousand people, and the sight of it unnerves me. I've never felt so small and insignificant as I do now.

Music pounds against my eardrums as the Westbridge band blares the fight song—one I vaguely recognize. I take a steady breath, then another, trying to keep my anxiety from spiraling.

I don't like crowds. And this is... a lot. The sea of gold and navy presses in from every direction. The energy is electric, raw, and untamed. Despite the spike of fear through me, I also feel a jolt of excitement.

And then I see him.

Hunter stands near the bench, dressed in team gear instead of his jersey—a quarter-zip pullover and joggers. He's mid-conversation with what looks like a reporter, large headphones resting over his ears, a microphone angled toward his mouth. He gestures with a clipboard in his hand, relaxed, confident. Happy.

Even from here, I can see the charm dialed up to a thousand. He laughs, eyes crinkling, and then something shifts. The reporter asks a question, and Hunter's expression turns serious as he shakes his head.

He hasn't noticed me yet, and it gives me a second to study him. In a way, knowing he's there grounds me.

A staffer guides me to my seat—directly behind the Westbridge bench. Like, literally behind it. I could reach out and touch the players if I wanted to. Which I don't, obviously... Except maybe one.

I sink into the plush black leather chair, heart pounding and aware of how out of place I probably look. I set my satchel at my feet and straighten just as a waiter approaches, placing another pristine bottle of Fiji water on the small table beside me. On the other side of the little table is another empty leather seat and part of me wonders if perhaps the new bottle is for whoever will be in that seat.

The waiter disappears, and I take in my surroundings. This is absurd. How many people would kill for this seat? To be this close to the action? To the players? I glance at the polished leather, the VIP lanyards, the catered water. This probably costs more than my yearly tuition.

My eyes flick back to Hunter. He looks untouchable out there. Larger than life beneath the lights. Fans hold up signs with his name and number scrawled across neon poster boards. One catches my eye:

Call me #13

A phone number scribbled underneath it. I flush. I have his number. He texted me. We hung out this morning. He bought me a book. I'm still slightly buzzing from the way he pulled my lip free from my teeth. But would he do that with anyone? Is that just... his way?

What do I know? I'm only his tutor. The thought lodges somewhere uncomfortable in my chest.

He removes the headset and shakes the reporter's hand. They exchange a few brief words before he starts heading toward the team bench... toward me. Butterflies swoon around in my stomach. Then, he sees me. And everything changes. His entire face lights up as his eyes lock in on me.

I rise automatically, smoothing down the jersey I'd had to cinch at the waist with a hair tie because on me, it's closer to a dress.

He's stopped twice on his way over, high-fiving teammates, nodding at staff, but his eyes keep finding me. Like he's tethered to me. By the time he reaches the bench, coaches are talking to him, but he murmurs something in response and steps around them. Straight to me.

"Hey, Short-Stack," he says, grin spreading slow and warm. "You actually made it." I can hear the excitement in his voice.

"I did," I confirm. "Try not to sound so shocked. I did bring a book though, just in case..."

He drops into the chair beside me and then grins like it's been weeks instead of hours since we last saw each other.

"I wouldn't expect anything less," he says. "But that's not what surprised me."

I raise my brow, confused.

"It's not even the fact that you actually showed up..." His eyes trail down my body, slow and deliberate. "It's the fit." He clears his throat. "Didn't think I'd see my number look that good courtside."

Heat creeps up my cheeks.

"Careful," I shoot back. "You're laying it on thicker than the nacho cheese guy out front."

He laughs, glancing at the two bottles of Fiji on the table. "Bougie water too? You went full VIP."

I chuckle settling back into the oversized leather seat. "Sure did. Fancy all the way."

The lights dim slightly just as the music kicks up—bass-heavy and aggressive. The floor thrums beneath my feet. The arena darkens, and the roar builds until it presses in on my ribs. My chest tightens as the vibrations, screams, and bass pound in my head. I feel like I can't breathe, but then a warm hand slides into mine. Firm. Grounding.

I look down, then up. Hunter's eyes find mine instantly.

"It's alright." he says, voice calm despite the chaos. How I can hear his voice so clearly through all the noise is beyond me. It's as if my brain knows he's safe and will protect me. "They're just getting ready to start." The pressure of his hand steadies me. My pulse slows.

I look back onto the court where players begin warm-up drills, sneakers squeaking against polished wood.

"So," I clear my throat. "Do I cheer now? Or is that premature?"

His mouth curves. "Only if you want be the girl who clapped for warm-ups."

My face warms as my nerves finally begin to settle. Hunter's humor grounds me.

"Tempting," I say. "I'm already standing out in your jersey, in the VIP section, with my very fancy water."

I glance at the court, overwhelmed all over again. I know absolutely nothing about this sport. "Okay, seriously," I sigh. "Are there rules? Or do I just... watch and hope I figure it out?"

He nods solemnly. "Pretty much. Just follow the ball and cheer when we score. Or when I yell something, because it's probably brilliant and game-changing."

I scoff. "Wow. Incredible guidance. You should coach." He grins and nudges my knee lightly with his.

"But seriously," he says, voice softening, "you're already doing great. Just being here? Supporting me? That's more than enough."

I blink. The sincerity in his tone catches me off guard. For a second, the noise fades and it's just us—close enough to feel the warmth of his body near mine. Before I can respond—

"Jace!"

A man in a Westbridge quarter-zip waves him over from the bench.

Hunter stands. "Ah, Coach Trent," he says under his breath. "Time to pretend I'm useful."

He flashes me a grin. "Make yourself comfortable, okay? I'll swing by." Then, with a teasing lift of his brow, "and don't just sip the fancy water. The lounge food's actually good. You deserve the full VIP experience."

And just like that, he's gone—jogging toward the bench, clipboard in hand, slipping seamlessly back into his world. I stare after him for maybe a second too long.

God. Even benched, he's charming. Thoughtful. And, completely disarming.

Who says, "you deserve the full VIP experience", and makes it sound like a genuine compliment and not a line from a smut book?

I shift in my seat, suddenly hyper-aware of the jersey on my body and the thundering arena around me. The lights flash overhead, and the noise spikes even louder. A deep, theatrical voice booms through the speakers:

"Westbridge Hawks fans...are you READY?"

The crowd detonates.

Music blares, spotlights whirl and I find myself lightly clapping along—awkward at first, trying to blend in. The players take the court to loud, thumping music, all momentum and warm from the drills. They huddle around a man who I assume is the head coach, arms slung over each other's shoulders for one final burst of unity.

Hunter doesn't join the circle. He paces the sideline beside Coach Trent, clipboard tucked under his arm, jaw tight. Focus radiates off him. And even though he's not playing, he's still fully in it. The envy in his eyes as he watches his teammates isn't lost on me.

Tip-off starts and the Hawks secure the ball, and Hunter's voice cuts through the chaos as he shouts instructions. He watches the court like a predator tracking movement. Each of his muscles is coiled and behaves like if he blinks, he'll miss something.

He's intense. Not the cocky, posturing kind of intense.

This is different. This is earned.

Coach Trent leans in, says something. Hunter nods sharply and cups his hands around his mouth, calling out to one of the guards.

He doesn't look at me once. Which is probably for the best. Because I am absolutely watching him... maybe a little too closely.

Midway through the first quarter, I realize my fingers have been fisted in the hem of his jersey. I slowly uncurl them.

I'm actually following the game now. Mostly. It didn't take me too long to figure it out. When a Westbridge player sinks a three, the arena erupts. Students nearly topple over each other in celebration. And I clap too, confident this time.

I can't help but smile as I watch Hunter, just as he looks back. A quick flick of his eyes over his shoulder. But they land on mine. Sharp. Knowing. Heat flashes between us like a struck match.

Hunter raises a brow, the corner of his mouth lifting in a smug little smirk. Then he turns back to the court, like nothing happened.

My face burns as I drop back into my seat. Awesome. Caught mid-clap like a starstruck idiot.

CHAPTER 9

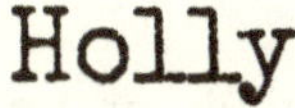

A BUZZER BLARES. THE scoreboard flashes.

WESTBRIDGE – 41

FULTON TECH – 38

The team pours off the court toward the tunnel. I glance after them, debating whether to stretch my legs in the VIP lounge or remain planted in my black throne of basketball virginity awkwardness. Before I can decide, Hunter appears. He crouches beside my seat like it's the most natural thing for a six-foot-nine man to fold himself in half.

"Halftime snack break," he says, flashing a grin. "I can join for a few minutes. VIP perks include warm cookies and judgment-free chili-cheese nachos."

My brows lift. "Well... when you say it like that..."

He extends a hand and I take it, letting him pull me to my feet.

"I'm surprised you're here at all," I admit as we walk. "Don't you have to go in with your team?"

Hunter rubs his chin in thought, "Well, I probably should. But Coach McGraw and Coach Trent don't want me overextending. They want me to be healthy so I can get back in the game faster." A small smirk curves at his lips. "So they don't mind me spending a few minutes with my 'special guest'."

Special guest.

I hesitate for a moment before asking the question that's been lodged in my throat. "What happened?" I say softly, and then quickly add, "If you don't mind me asking."

His expression shifts. He exhales slowly as he runs a hand through his dark hair. "It was just a hit," he says. "Bad angle. Bad timing."

I wait a moment hoping he'll say more. When he doesn't, I decide not to probe any further. In a few long strides, Hunter leads me into the VIP lounge. The second we enter, heads turn. Some eyes widen at the sight of Hunter. A ripple of cheers, handshakes, pats on the back, well-wishes erupts in the room. It takes a minute to untangle from the small swarm.

Eventually, he leads me to a small tucked-away table in a corner. He orders chili-cheese nachos and I ask for a Diet Coke. When the food arrives, we share the nachos, and they're every bit as delicious as they look. I groan softly at the first bite—sour cream, avocado, and salsa with perfectly crisp nachos.

"I can't believe this exists in the same building as the basketball court." I say, laughing.

Hunter grins. "I told you. Hawks Arena may be chaos, but the lounge? Classy."

He grabs a heavily-loaded chip, barely managing to fit it into his mouth. I try not to stare, but fail. I then take one myself, moaning at the flavorful, cheesy-goodness of it.

"Is this a pre-approved training meal?" I tease.

"Absolutely not," he replies with a mouthful. "But I'm benched, remember? One chip won't kill me."

I glance at the towering stack in his hand. "That looks more like three chips in one."

He laughs and I laugh with him. It hits me suddenly how easy this feels. How much I've been smiling tonight. Hunter's relaxed—sleeves rolled up, hair slightly mussed from repeatedly dragging his hands through it during the first half.

After a few moments, he says, softer this time, "I'm glad you came."

The words land differently. Not flirty. Not teasing. Just... honest. "Yeah," I reply, meeting his eyes. "Me too." And I mean it more than I expected to.

We fall into a comfortable silence, the kind that settles warmly between two people beginning to get comfortable in each other's orbit. It's... nice. I take a sip of my soda while Hunter attempts to pull apart a chip from the stack. The cheese stretches dramatically between the chip and plate.

"Okay," he mutters, grinning, "this might be a choking hazard." He pulls the molten strand free and shoves the bite into his mouth. I stare at his lips for a little too long.

Stop staring. Snap out of it.

"So," I say clearing my throat, "do your parents come to your games a lot? Or any siblings?"

He swallows, brow creasing slightly at the shift. "My parents come when they can. They're not here tonight because I'm benched, but if they're not in the stands, they're usually watching from home." He gives a small shrug. "And no siblings. Just me. What about you?"

"Do my parents come watch me play basketball?" I deadpan. "Um... no."

He laughs. "You know what I mean. Siblings? What about your parents?"

I tilt my head, thinking. "I have two siblings. An older brother, and a younger sister who's still in high school. Mom's a teacher, dad's an accountant." I hesitate for a second. "I think my family's a little socially awkward, so, I don't see or talk to them much. I'm mostly on my own."

He studies me for a moment. "I get that," he says. It's quieter, almost sympathetic. Then his mouth curves, just enough to lighten it. "Well, I'm more than happy to keep you company."

My heart stutters, and I feel a blush creeping up my face. "Um..." I think for a moment and finally manage, "thanks. I think I might like that."

He grins, and my pulse kicks up all over again.

"Good."

A few minutes later, he heads back to the bench to help prepare for the second half. I linger long enough to finish off a few more nachos and make a quick stop in the VIP lounge bathroom before returning to my seat.

The second half begins with the same explosive energy, but this time, the tip-off goes to Fulton Tech. The teams trade baskets, with the crowd roaring in the background. But, slowly the Hawks start to slip. Hunter is on his feet beside Coach Trent, shouting instructions, jaw tight. The head coach rotates players in and out. Fouls stack up, and the crown momentum shifts a little. I don't understand it all, but I understand the tension. With thirty seconds left, the Hawks trail by eight points.

I rise from my seat without realizing it, the anxious energy buzzing under my skin. My teeth catch my lip as the Hawks fight back. Now they're within one. The arena shakes with energy.

Hunter doesn't look at me once. He's locked in, every muscle taut. Even from the sidelines, his competitiveness radiates off him. He wants to be out there. I can see it.

The clock ticks down.

Fulton Tech launches a desperate shot at the buzzer, and it drops. Silence ripples through the arena before the visiting section erupts. Game Over. The Hawks lose.

Disappointment settles heavy in the air as people begin to file out. I sink back into my seat, a ridiculous thought flickering through me. Was I bad luck?

Unsure what to do, I stay in my luxurious chair. The teams exchange quick handshakes before heading toward the tunnel, shoulders squared despite the loss. Hunter lingers a second more.

Then, he turns, finally seeming to remember me.

"Give me a few minutes," he says forcing a smile that doesn't reach his eyes. "I'll meet you outside."

I just nod. I slip out of the arena the way I came. The energy outside is muted now—some parties are still continuing, but the earlier frenzy is dulled by the loss.

The night air hits my face—cool and heavy.

Most of the tailgates have packed up. The crowds thin into clusters of students debating after-parties. I find a bench beneath a streetlamp and sit, unsure how long I'll actually be waiting.

The longer I sit, the colder I get. I left my jacket in my dorm, and I regret it now. To distract myself, I pull out my book and read beneath the yellow glow of the lamp. By the time I glance up again, nearly half an hour has passed. The arena grounds are mostly empty now. Eventually, a few towering figures emerge form the tunnel. They seem to be in high spirits, laughing as they leave.

Then one of them separates from the group. Even in shadow, I know it's him. Hunter steps into the light, that easy smile back on his face. "Hey, Short-Stack. Sorry that took longer than I thought. I wasn't sure if you'd still be here."

I stand, sliding my book back into my bag. "Well, my butt is almost completely frozen to the bench, but otherwise... I'm fine."

His gaze sweeps the nearly deserted plaza.

"Shit, it is freezing out here." He rubs the back of his neck. "Let me take you back to my place. Falconer Hall. You can warm up for a bit, then I'll walk you to your dorm."

His place. His room?

My heart stutters. I should've realized he lives in Falconer. It's the all-male dorm closest to the athletic facilities. A lot of the athletes live there. Especially those on scholarships, which, I assume Hunter is.

I hesitate just long enough to acknowledge the choice.

"Alright," I say slowly.

Hunter leads the way, but it's only a short walk. A few steps, really. We walk side by side in easy silence. Maybe he's still processing the loss. Maybe he needs a breather after that roller coaster of a game.

"So… maybe I shouldn't come to any more games?" I ask lightly. Mostly.

He frowns and turns toward me. "Why would you say that?"

"Well, you guys lost the game… and it was my first time there. Maybe I'm bad luck."

He stops walking and turns fully to face me. "Holly," he says, like the idea genuinely bothers him. "We lost because we couldn't make free throws. Not because you were in the stands." He leans down, his voice lowers just a little. "And for the record, having you there was the only part of tonight that didn't suck."

Heat returns to my cheeks, before I can stop it. I grin idiotically at his words.

We reach the glass doors of Falconer Hall just as a sharp gust of wind slices through my jersey. I hunch into myself, arms folding instinctively. He notices immediately and swipes his ID. The door clicks, unlocking.

"Come on," he says, holding the door open for me. "Let's get you warmed up." The warmth hits the second I step inside. It feels almost unreal after the cold—like walking straight into a blanket.

Falconer looks exactly how I imagined it: dark wood trim, framed photos of past athletic teams lining the walls, muted lighting; very masculine and old-school. He leads me across the quiet lobby toward another set of secured doors. A quick swipe of his card and they click open.

The layout of the dormitory is relatively similar to mine— the same maze of hallways and stairs as Meadowbrooke—but everything feels slightly bigger. Broader.

Hunter takes the stairs two at a time. I do not. I can't. By the second flight, I'm trying not to audibly wheeze behind him.

He notices me lagging behind and stops. "Sorry, Short-Stack. I'm not used to having company."

"It's... fine," I huff as I catch up, no longer cold—just overly sweaty. My legs feel like overcooked noodles.

Hunter quirks a brow. "Want me to carry you?" I glare and he chuckles.

"Alright, noted." He lifts his hands up in surrender. We climb the remaining steps to the fourth floor. His room is the last one on the left. Room 430. Plain wooden door, no decorations. No personality spilling into the hallway like the girl's dorm.

He unlocks it and steps aside. "After you."

I walk in slowly. The room is single occupancy like mine, yet it feels entirely different. Navy walls. Dark oak furniture. His bed is extra long, neatly made with a solid navy comforter tucked tight.

I hear the door shut behind me with a soft click.

The room is tidy, unexpectedly so. A laptop sits on his desk, and a couple of textbooks stack beside it. Floating shelves hover above with more books and notebooks. *Of Mice and Men* peeks out from the row, which makes me blink. There's shelf with a few basketball trophies and medals, and framed photo rests near them—Hunter standing between an older man and woman, both smiling proudly. His parents, I assume.

Behind his laptop sits a jar of peanut M&Ms and I can't help but stifle a laugh. Over his bed hangs a signed, black-framed Kevin Garnett jersey—Number 21—white and forest-green in a sleek black frame. It's the only color in the room that doesn't belong to Westbridge.

I hadn't realized I was staring until I inhale. It smells like him. Not like sweat or gym socks like I expected from the men's dorm. But it's different. Clean, warm and something sharp underneath—amber and cedar and fresh air after rain. Subtle. Controlled. Like him.

As he approaches me, the scent deepens. Hunter hands me a navy Westbridge sweatshirt. "Here," he says. "For the walk home."

I blink up at him. " Oh. Thank you."

The fabric is soft. Warm from where it's been folded, sitting in his room. It smells unmistakably like him. I want to inhale it, roll in it, but refrain. I press it to my chest for a second longer than necessary before pulling it on. He smirks as if he knew where my mind went.

The sweatshirt swallows me whole. The sleeves dangle well past my fingertips, the hem grazes just below my knees—layered over the jersey, I look like a walking Westbridge advertisement. Although, I guess I already was wearing Hunter's jersey.

I roll the sleeves up, fumbling slightly, well aware of his eyes scanning me. I don't miss the way his expression shifts. His gaze drags slowly down, then back up again.

"You look better in it than I do," he murmurs.

A blush creeps up my face. I scoff lightly, "You say that like I don't look ridiculous."

His mouth curves, but his eyes don't soften. "No," he says softly. "You don't look ridiculous." He inhales deeply. "You look like mine in it."

My brain freezes. A warmth shoots straight through me traveling down my belly. I open my mouth to come up with something clever, but then close it. I have no idea how to react. No witty response. Somewhere lodged between my lungs and heart, my stomach flutters before blooming like wildfire. I open my mouth again still at a loss of words. But, he chuckles. It's low, and I can barely hear the huff beneath his breath. "Let's go before I don't let you."

CHAPTER 10

Hunter

THE MOMENT I WALKED into Room E, I knew.

It wasn't just the way her eyes flicked around the study room like she was pretending this was still casual. It wasn't even the way her arms were crossed as she sat stiffly in her seat, laptop open, notebook and pen perfectly aligned beside it—pretending to be mad at me for being ten minutes late.

It was the smell.

Faint. Warm. Familiar.

That subtle mix of spice and cedar that usually clings to me after a shower—it was on her now. In her hair. In her clothes. I didn't need to see the sweatshirt to know she'd been wearing it. And that fact alone made it nearly impossible to focus. The idea of her curled up in it. Probably sleeping in it. Wrapped in something that had once been against my skin. My sweatshirt has now felt that creamy skin, bare—before *me*. As if those filthy dreams of all the ways I want her weren't enough to torment me.

The room suddenly feels too small as I take the chair across from her and start unpacking my notebook, pen, and *Much Ado About Nothing*. I try to keep myself busy. Don't stare too long. Don't lean. Don't breathe in too deeply. Because if I do, I'll catch that blend of Dior Sauvage and her warm vanilla again, and my mind will go exactly where it shouldn't.

You have no idea what smelling my cologne on you does to me.

Don't get a fucking boner with all my dirty thoughts. Christ, this is more difficult that I thought.

Even though she isn't wearing the sweatshirt now, I think of all the times it clung to me after a workout or after an early-morning run. How I didn't wash it as often as I should've. It definitely wasn't washed when I gave it to her—but, it wasn't "dirty" at least. I can still picture it swallowing her whole that night in my dorm room. The sleeves drowning her hands. The hem brushing just above her thighs. It was adorable. She was adorable. *Mine*.

The thought hits harder than it should. I swallow it down.

I grab my backpack and pull out my assignment, sliding it across the table.

Holly leans in to look at it. "This the assignment for the week?" she asks, tucking a strand of her short hair from the front of her glasses behind her ear. I lean in too, closer than necessary. Our fingers meet as she reaches for the paper. Not an accident.

She blinks, but doesn't pull away. Neither do I. Her large, hazel, doe-eyes lift to mine, shining brightly beneath her glasses. The fluorescent lights magnify the little flecks of green in her eyes. The air feels still.

"It is..." I reply, my voice lower than intended. I curl my fingers lightly, brushing hers again. It's soft, barely a touch, just a teasing pass to see her response. Enough to feel the heat.

She pauses—for a moment, enough to acknowledge it—before drawing the paper toward her, and clearing her throat. She begins reading the questions like nothing happened.

I match her calm ignoring the pounding of my heart. We move through the hour like that. Flipping pages, scribbling notes, brushing hands as we pass things back and forth. At one point, we reach for the highlighter at the same time. Our hands overlap fully this time—palm to palm. She inhales. I feel it. But she doesn't move. Neither do I. Just for a second too long. Then she pulls back and continues outlining the scene.

"And you feel alright with your upcoming read?" she asks, eyes on the page. "I know you missed a few classes..." Her voice snaps me out of my stupor.

I clear my throat, sitting straighter. "Yeah. *A Comedy of Errors*. I've started it, but I'm playing catch-up."

It's an understatement. I'm playing "catch-up" in so many ways. One being my brain not losing my mind every time her hand touches mine.

She nods. "Well, let me know if you need help before our next session. You have my number." Her voice is quiet, shy. Like she wants me to text her.

I grin, because I'd like nothing more than to text her night and day.

"Yeah, absolutely." I say. "I appreciate it."

Once the hour is up, we both stand packing our things almost too slowly. A part of me wants to linger... to take her deep into the stacks and possess her. It wouldn't be difficult. The library, especially in this area, is empty. Private.

We walk toward the front in silence and I breathe in her smell with every step. She's small beside me, barely reaching my chest. Holly looks up at me and offers a tiny smile. It hits harder than it should. I swallow, forcing my brain to cooperate. I try to clear my head—think of something normal to say.

"I've been cleared to play again." I finally sputter. My voice comes out rougher than I wanted to. "Coach McGraw plans to put me in tomorrow."

Her expression shifts as her smile deepens.

"You should come, since we're home again. I can hook you up with those VIP tickets." I croon, hoping she'll say yes—more like, praying.

She smirks. "Are you sure you want me there? Last time I came, you guys lost. I don't want to be bad luck."

I scoff. "I told you. That was because we missed free throws." How can she be so superstitious? And why do I find it so adorable? Then I add, "and we won't lose."

She quirks a suspicious brow. "Why not?"

I grin, unable to stop it. "Because I'll be back on the court, Short-Stack."

I wink. She rolls her eyes but her expression shifts almost immediately, this time her gaze piercing hard. "But seriously, are you sure you're ready? It hasn't been that long since you collapsed..." Her voice trails off. There it is. The real question. I'd hoped my vague answer on Saturday would've been enough. Clearly, it wasn't.

I've been pretending it didn't happen. Pretending that I didn't collapse on national television from a freak accident of a hard-foul. That my heart didn't stop for a moment and that I hadn't almost died. This fucking condition...

Every interview since has asked me about it. Their "thoughts and prayers" are with me. I've gotten good at giving safe answers.

But Holly isn't a reporter.

The truth presses at the back of my throat.

So, I offer her what I'm comfortable sharing. "It was a freak hit, Stacks," I try to lighten the air. "But I'm okay. Mentally, physically, I'm fine. Doctors made sure everything was alright and cleared me. They're comfortable with me playing."

That part is true. Mostly.

Holly studies me like she's trying to read between the lines. Then, she exhales as if she lost a mental debate. "I'd love to see you play," she admits with a shy smile. "I just..."

I stop walking and turn Holly to face me.

"What Holly?" My voice lowers. Not demanding, but steady. "You just what?" It's a reassuring whisper that she can confide in me. I lean over, bringing my face close to hers.

She looks up at me, and her eyes are softer now. Softer than I'd ever seen them.

"...I don't think I can see that happen to you again."

Her voice is barely audible, but it hits me like a punch to the chest. Not dramatic. Not exaggerated. Just real. For a second, I don't know what to do with that. I let the silence sit between us. Then, I tilt my head and let a small grin tug at my mouth.

"You starting to catch feelings for me?" I murmur.

Her eyes narrow instantly, and she swats my arm. But that pink bloom across her cheeks gives her away. "Don't flatter yourself," she says, turning and walking toward the front of the library.

"Too late," I grin, falling into step beside her. "You're probably already picturing me walking through some misty field, shirt unbuttoned, staring broodingly into the distance."

She stops walking so abruptly I nearly walk into her. The glare she gives me could scorch the earth. "Absolutely not," she huffs.

I bite back a laugh. It's like I just insulted Jane Austen herself.

"Oh, come on," I nudge her lightly with my elbow. Hoping I can get something out of her. "You're telling me you haven't mentally cast me as your modern-day Mr. Darcy?"

"You're more of a Wickham," she snaps without hesitation.

"Ouch," I fake gasp. "I don't know who that is, but it sounds rude."

Her smirk is lethal. She turns again, and her short hair swings around, catching the faint smell of my cologne and throwing it right back at me. My heart does that stupid flip again.

"So, I'll see you at 7:30?" I call after her watching her hips sway as she walks away. She pauses at the double doors, glancing over her shoulder.

"See you there." She turns on her heel and leaves me as she exits.

I can't help that little fist-pump before I leave toward the arena.

CHAPTER 11

Holly

I ARRIVE AT HAWK'S Arena same way I did last time—flustered and overwhelmed by all the sheer number of people. At least now I know where I'm going. I navigate straight to the VIP lounge without the salmon-swimming-upstream ordeal.

Tonight, I'm dressed differently though. An old-gold pleated skirt, a navy, slouchy cardigan, and a white cami underneath. I didn't want to feel like I didn't belong in the VIP lounge with all the executive-looking types.

I appreciate Hunter trying to protect me from the chaos of the crowd, especially since I was here by myself, but how many times can he give me these VIP tickets? Surely, there's a limit. Don't other players use them for family and friends? And yet, here I am again. I feel a bit spoiled.

For tonight's game, I ordered a salted soft-pretzel and—on impulse—an amaretto sour. I'm not usually a hard liquor kind of girl, but, when in Rome... Or, I guess, when in the VIP lounge.

The bartender slides the drink toward me, amber and elegant in its low-ball glass. I take my pretzel and make my way to the courtside seat—the same one as last time. It already feels familiar. I settle in and immediately spot him.

Hunter's in his white jersey tonight, navy-and-gold stripes down the sides. He's at the free-throw line, methodical and controlled. Throw after throw, repetition after repetition. He's a natural—back in his element. He hasn't missed a beat. A sense of pride rises in me as I watch him.

I lift my drink to my lips, eyeing him over the rim of the glass. He looks effortless and alive tonight, not like someone who was hospitalized a couple weeks ago.

His muscles flex as he pivots, and releases another shot. And boy does my heart thud as I watch all those cuts. The sleeveless jersey. The compression sleeve hugging his right arm. The confidence that radiates off him as he moves.

I internally groan as I tear off another piece of my pretzel, trying to look casual. When he jogs to the bench for a hydration break, he spots me almost instantly.

A big smile sprawls across his face. "Hey, Short-Stack. Glad you made it."

My heart skips another beat as the heat climbs up my neck.

"Me too," I reply, softer than I meant to.

His gaze drifts to the glass on my table and he quirks a brow. "What you got there?" His voice teasing, curious.

"Amaretto Sour." I say, trying to sound confident. Failing miserably.

"Huh," he chuckles. "Didn't picture you as an amaretto sour kind of girl but," he pauses and leans a bit closer, "I like it. Enjoy it, Stacks."

And then he winks. Actually winks before jogging back toward the court like he didn't just short circuit my entire system. Talk about a thirst-trap.

I grab my amaretto sour and take another sip—a larger one—and then put it down.

The players disappear into the tunnel as the lights dim. Bass-heavy music floods the arena, vibrating through the floor and up my spine.

The announcer's voice booms. "Tonight, the Westbridge Hawks take on the Appalachian U Mountaineers!"

The crowd explodes with boos and claps in a conflicting chorus. When the lights go off, a promo for Westbridge plays. A hype video flashes across the massive screens overhead. Slow-motion highlights. Dramatic lighting. Muscles, sweat, victory poses. Hunter's image lights up the screens. Close-up, focused, his jaw tight and eyes intense. I can't help but feel a little tickle of pride as I watch him.

The arena on the other hand loses its mind. The screams are immediate—high-pitched, ecstatic. A cluster of girls near the student section practically leap over one another. A few cheerleaders shout, "we love you, Hunter!"

My fingers tighten around my pretzel. A sharp twinge of jealousy sparks low in my chest. It's ridiculous. Of course they scream for him. He's the star. I'm just—

I take another sip of my drink and push the thought away.

Then the announcer starts calling our team. Numbers first, then their names.

The crowd goes absolutely feral when they call, "Number Thirteen... Hunter Jace!"

The man comes jogging out like a God—a gladiator about to take his place in history, re-entering the arena for the first time since his absence. The noise is deafening, but I can't help but stare at Hunter.

When he runs past the bench, he turns—just for second—and points straight at me. And winks. My heart stutters and my mouth goes dry. Before I realize it, the camera pans over to me and suddenly my image appears on the Jumbotron. My eyes go wide. I clap immediately in embarrassment hopefully to draw the attention off me.

I never thought that Hunter's shine might spill onto me.

VIP seats are one thing. But, being publicly associated with the star player? That's attention on the whole another level. Attention that I'm not sure I'm ready for.

I gulp, as I sink in my seat taking another sip of my drink. Hunter's completely locked onto the court.

I'm not sure he has the slightest idea of what he's done to me. Even if he had, he doesn't show it.

The announcer finishes the roster and the team takes their place. It's Hunter in the center circle. His six-foot-nine stature makes him the obvious choice.

The whistle blows and he leaps. Clean contact.

My eyes follow him as he goes back and forth. He makes it look easy, like running isn't something he does, it's something he is. I can't help but smile.

Watching him in person is nothing like watching him on my laptop. In the arena, he feels bigger, sharper, more focused. He's playing with the intent to win.

For someone so tall, his coordination is unreal. He's fast, nimble even—surprisingly so. He doesn't even have to leap half the time—just extend a long, muscular arm and pretty much drop the ball in.

When he sinks another shot, I clap without thinking. Then, right before the halftime buzzer, he launches a long-range shot. The ball arcs. Swish. The buzzer sounds. The arena explodes. And, I jump out of my luxury chair and shout, like I've been doing this my whole life.

Halftime:

WESTBRIDGE – 55 APPALACHIAN U – 42

I'm still buzzing as I turn toward the lounge. But as I do, arms wrap around me from behind. Warm and solid, slightly damp with sweat. I gasp.

Hunter pulls me into a quick hug and presses a fast, breathless kiss to my cheek.

"Be right back," he murmurs against my skin.

And just like that, he's gone. Running with his teammates through the tunnel.

I'm frozen... breathless. My cheek tingles and instinctively my fingers graze it.

He kissed me. In public. In front of thousands of people.

Heat rushes up my face as reality catches up.

I force myself toward the VIP lounge and immediately slip into the bathroom, locking myself inside one of the stalls.

My hand again rises to my cheek. Why did he kiss me? Adrenaline? Like that photo—V-J Day in Time Square—when the sailor kisses the woman on the street?

Or was it something else? Have the looks really meant something? The teasing; the flirting? The way he touches my hand a second too long?

I press my lips together, trying to calm my heart.

I don't do this. I don't get swept up by star athletes and halftime kisses. I don't get chosen. And yet, he ran straight to me.

Gathering myself, I splash cool water on my wrists and cheeks before going to order popcorn and a bottle of water and heading back to my seat to watch the second half.

The second half mirrors the first. Hunter wins the tip again and passes it off to his teammate.

From there, it's obvious—Westbridge is stronger. Appalachian makes a hard push, but they can't quiet close the gap. Every time they inch forward, Hunter or one of the others answers back. There's a rhythm to it now. A dominance.

When the final buzzer sounds, the arena is filled with a fresh surge of celebration.

Confetti canons explode overhead. The student section charges the court. Music blares. Strangers hug each other like they've survived something monumental.

I'm unsure if this is normal, but I stay in my plush leather seat until the crowd starts to dwindle a bit.

I scan the chaos for him. A flash of black hair with headphones catches my eye. He's mid-interview, smiling and laughing into a reporter's camera like this is the most natural thing in the world.

A blonde cheerleader rushes up beside him, throwing her arms around his waist.

My breath catches. She's gorgeous. He drapes an arm loosely around her, but his attention stays on the reporter. He doesn't look down at her. Still. My chest tightens, heart pounding as I watch him.

This is his world. Loud. Bright. Public.

Is there really space for someone like me? Is this really a world I could belong in?

I swallow. Maybe I let myself get carried away. Maybe a halftime kiss doesn't mean anything in a place like this.

The arena starts to thin out, but the court is still crowded. Maybe it's easier if I just leave.

I take another deep breath, and stand to make my way toward the VIP lounge exit. My hand reaches for the door handle, and suddenly, warm fingers wrap around my wrist. I turn to see Hunter smiling down at me.

"You leaving?" He asks lightly, but the teasing fades as he studies my expression.

"I... you seemed busy," I say, forcing a small smile. "I didn't want you to feel like you had to tend to me. Good game, by the way."

His brows furrow slightly, but then chuckles. "I'd give anything to tend to you."

"It's just..." My voice softens, "I saw you with that cheerleader and—"

He looks at me, confused for a moment before realizing what I was referring to. Hunter's eyes widen. "Fuck no. Tammie-Lee..." a short laugh escapes him. "Holly, no. She's been around the program for years. She hugs everyone. I barely registered it." He steps closer, lowering his voice. "Honestly? For a second, I thought it was you."

My pulse spikes.

His expression shifts before his eyes glisten with mischief. "Don't leave," he says. "I'll give you the backstage tour. We just have to wait until the locker room clears out."

I hesitate, searching his face for any insincerity. When I don't immediately acquiesce, Hunter gives me large, brown, puppy-dog eyes.

"Please," he adds quickly. "I promise I'll make it worth your while."

I sigh, ultimately giving in. "Okay... I can wait."

Hunter smiles, satisfaction flickering in his eyes.

"Good girl." He leans in, whispering in my ear. His breath makes a shiver trail down my spine. My mouth suddenly feels dry. It elicits some unfamiliar feeling within me. "Now, go sit in your cozy chair, and I'll come get you in a few minutes."

My mouth opens, tongue darting out to lick my dry lips. "Okay," I manage.

He winks before disappearing through the tunnel.

I plop down, all hot and bothered—heated, waiting for the return of my Mr. Darcy.

CHAPTER 12

Holly

I SINK DEEPER INTO the plush leather of the VIP lounge chair, arms crossed tight across my chest in a weak attempt at self-regulation. The game is long over. The crowd has cleared. Only a few stragglers linger along the lower ring of the arena, while the staff sweep confetti into piles.

And, me?

I haven't moved. Hot, restless, and clinging to my wristlet, trying not to combust—waiting for Hunter's return.

When he finally appears, my breath eases a bit.

Hair damp from the shower. Westbridge hoodie, and, sweet mercy—gray sweatpants. Low-slung gray sweatpants. The kind of sweatpants that should come with a warning label.

"Sorry to keep you waiting," he says, voice deeper now, post-shower husky. "You ready for the tour?"

No, sir, I am not ready for this.

But I nod, anyway.

He holds out his hand. "Come on, Short-Stack. Time to show you where the magic happens."

I take it. His palm is warm and solid around mine as he leads me across the court and through the tunnel. Without the screaming fans and bass-heavy music, it feels different. Intimate.

The hallway is industrial, with concrete floors, exposed pipes, and fluorescent lights. We stop at the athletic gym first. State-of-the-art equipment—treadmills, free weights, and other things I'm unfamiliar with—lines the walls. In the corner, there's a fridge stocked with protein drinks and energy drinks. I raise a brow at the weight loaded on one of the barbels. I wonder if they can actually lift that much... or if he can.

From there, he leads me past their practice court. Not as lavish as the main arenas—simple oak wood, white boundary lines, and racks of basketballs neatly lined up along the wall.

"Want to take a shot?" he asks casually. He saunters over to one of the racks, grabs a ball, and dribbles it back toward me with easy confidence before holding it out.

"Are you serious?" I laugh. "Look how short I am."

His eyes drift slowly down my petite form, and I swallow.

"I bet you can make it," he says, voice full of confidence.

I give him a wary look but I take the basketball from his hand. It feels too big for me. Everything about this feels too big for me. I walk to the free-throw line and tilt my head back to stare at the hoop. Wow... it's so much higher than I realized.

I feel Hunter behind me. His cologne lingering. That cologne I've been mildly obsessed with since he gave me his sweatshirt. The sweatshirt that is still very much in my possession.

I dribble the ball awkwardly a couple times, the sound echoing in the empty gym. My palms are already sweaty. I exhale, bend my knees, and suddenly strong hands grip my waist. Before I can process what's happening, I'm lifted clean off the floor.

A startled squeal escapes my lips, followed by a giggle as the world shifts and the rim is suddenly right there—within reach.

"Shoot," he instructs.

I toss the ball forward, and it drops straight through the net with a soft swish. He lowers me slowly, deliberately against his strong body, until my feet touch the hardwood again. His hands linger on my waist, his fingers gently brushing against the fabric of my sweater, sending a dizzying wave through me.

"Told you you could make it," he rumbles near my ear.

The vibration of his voice against my skin sends a shiver down my spine. There's a quiet pause as I adjust my tiny skirt and cardigan, which had slipped off my shoulder revealing the thin strap of my white cami. I tug it back up, feeling his gaze follow the movement. When I glance up at him, his eyes have darkened—hungry with lust. My cheeks flush, heat crawling up my neck.

"Pretty sure it's called an assist," I reply, my voice coming out lower than I intended.

Hunter's grin widens into that megawatt smile. "Look at you using a basketball term."

He reaches up and gently tucks a loose strand of hair behind my ear. The brush of his fingers is slow, unhurried, and the simple touch sends a flutter straight down my stomach. He lets his fingers trail just slightly as he pulls away, like he's testing the space between us. Then, as if nothing happened, he steps back.

"Come on," he says, voice smooth again. "I've got one last stop on the tour."

Hunter leads me down the industrial hallway. The silence between us is not uncomfortable. It hums as if we're both replaying that moment on the court. He stops in front of a wooden door and I mimic his tracks. I glance up at the plaque.

HAWKS LOCKER ROOM

"This is it," Hunter says. "The grand finale. Home team locker room. Where all the pre-game magic happens." He pushes the door open and gestures for me to go first. I hesitate, expecting lingering players and instant humiliation, but step inside anyway.

The space is nothing like I imagined.

Instead of sweat and chaos, it's sleek and modern. Black leather couches form a lounge area around a massive projected screen. A ping pong table sits off to one side. The lighting is soft yet masculine. There's even a fully stocked fridge and snack station lined with protein bars, fruit, and neatly arranged containers of prepped meals. It looks more like an upscale sports lounge than a locker room.

"Wow," I breathe. "And I thought the VIP lounge was bougie."

Hunter chuckles, "It's pretty nice, yeah. They've done a lot of remodeling over the past couple of years."

"Hawthorne could use a nice remodel like this," I joke as I circle around the ping pong table. "The library still looks like it's stuck in the eighties."

"You know what they say," Hunter replies lazily, "education is nowhere as important as basketball."

I shoot him a murderous glare. He just smiles—satisfied—until my scowls melts into a reluctant grin. He loves provoking me. I turn away before he sees how easily he can push my buttons. My eyes land on another large door to the left of the recreational room.

"What's in here?" I ask, I head toward it.

His eyes track me—slow and intent. "The locker room and showers."

He prowls toward me and my back presses against the door as he towers over me. Before I even realize, the door is swings open behind my weight. I gasp as I stumble backward. Hunter quickly reaches his long arm around to catch me, wrapping me tightly against his firm, muscled body, while his other arm firmly holds onto the door frame.

For a moment, we're frozen against each other—my back half-tilted into the doorway, my heart pounding in my throat. Hunter looks calm as ever while his grip tightens just slightly. I am a puddling mess within his grasp.

He shifts us upright, but he doesn't let go. Wordlessly, he moves us backward, slow and controlled. My eyes are locked on his, unable to look away. My breathing gets heavy as we step in tandem, silent, our faces mere inches. I don't know where he's guiding me; I just know I'm not afraid.

When my back hits another hard surface, a soft gasp escapes me. His thumb gently traces along my side, slipping beneath the edge of my cami, brushing my bare skin. Goosebumps rise instantly. His other hand slides up to the back of my neck, fingers threading into the short strands there, tilting my face up to his.

My chest heaves in and out rapidly as I stand there speechless within his grasp.

He's so damn tall and I feel impossibly small against him.

Hunter lowers his face, stopping just shy of my lips. I can feel the warmth of his breath. I can smell the clean, sharp edge of his cologne. It wraps around me, dizzying.

"Why do you feel so good against me, Holly?" he whispers against my mouth.

I shake my head, breathless. I don't know. I don't know why my entire body feels electrified in his hands. I don't know why he feels inevitable.

"I can't stop thinking about you," he admits, a faint grin brushing my lips. "Tell me you feel it too."

"Inexplicably so," I breathe.

That's all the permission he needs. The next second, Hunter crashes his mouth onto mine. It's hungry and desperate. He tastes like mint and heat and something entirely him. My mind spins as his body presses closer, overwhelming in the most intoxicating way. His long fingers tighten at my waist and I clutch at the front of his sweatshirt, pulling him closer.

His tongue thrusts deeper, tangling with mine and unexpectedly, a moan escapes me. Heat flares up my neck and cheeks as I instinctively try to pull back, embarrassed by the sound that escaped me.

"No, baby," he murmurs against my mouth, his voice low and rough. "I want all your moans. Let me have them."

The way he says it makes my knees weaken and my panties wet.

And, then I feel it. Feel *him*. Through those soft gray sweatpants, a hard rod presses against the outside of my skirt, and my mind spirals. Oh shit, he's huge.

I exhale shakily as my hands slide down his chest. Hunter's arms tighten around me, possessing me. Yet they feel soft somehow. His fingers skim across my thighs, teasing at the hem of my skirt. Every inch of skin he touches tingles.

We pause barely, our lips still close and breaths mingled. There's a silent understanding between us as Hunter continues to brush his fingers along my thigh as I tug at the bottom of his sweatshirt. Those dark brown eyes are filled with lust and yearning, piercing me to my core. I bite my lower lip, anticipation crackling in the space between us.

Then, without warning, he grabs my hand firmly. As if he's made a decision.

He leads me out of the locker room, long strides eating up the distance, his grip warm and steady. He knows exactly where he's taking me.

CHAPTER 13

Holly

WORDLESSLY, HUNTER LEADS ME into his dorm room, shutting the door behind us and locking it with a soft click. The entire walk from the arena to Falconer has been silent, desperate.

Now, in his private space—his room—my heart thuds faster than it ever has. Anticipation swells inside me. We stare at each other as he slowly guides me farther into his room, his overwhelming presence effortlessly steering me where he wants.

Those warm eyes, filled with want and desire, never leave mine. My breath hitches as I read them, see the yearning there. Suddenly, my clothes feel too tight, too warm against my skin as I stand there, motionless.

I've never done this before. A kiss, sure, a meaningless peck here and there. But nothing like this. Nothing that felt this consuming. It's only been a couple weeks, but somehow, Hunter has worked his way beneath my skin. He's made me feel seen. He makes me feel sexy—even. Especially now as he looks at me. Like he wants nothing more than to devour me. A hawk eyeing its prey.

He steps closer, slow and deliberate, like he knows I'm just one breath away from shattering. His fingers brush over the buttons of my cardigan, pausing at the top before sliding up the column of my throat and tracing along my jaw. A breath catches in my throat—my eyes flutter closed.

"I need you to tell me if you really want this," he says softly, his voice barely more than a rasp. "You can't tell me with just that look. I need the words. Because once we start, there's no going back. I won't be able to stop myself."

My heart pounds so hard I feel it in my ears. I nod at first. Then I swallow and force the words out.

"I want this," I breathe, reaching for the hem of his sweatshirt and curling my fingers into the fabric. "I want you."

His mouth is on mine instantly—not rough, just hungry. His hands cup my face like I'm something precious while his lips move over mine as if he's been starving for weeks.

I fumble with the hem of his sweatshirt, trying to tug it up, but he's so tall. My hands shake, and he pauses when he notices.

"Let me," he murmurs.

In one swift motion, he pulls off both his sweatshirt and t-shirt, leaving nothing but sculpted abs and those low-slung gray sweatpants that make my mouth go dry. I take him in slowly, openly admiring the athletic lines of his body. He's stunning. It's unfair, honestly. My hands itch to touch him. He looks almost unreal. How does someone even look like this? I stand there shamelessly ogling the man, my mouth watering at the sight.

"Hunter."

His name leaves my lips like a prayer to the gods—one I could whisper over and over without ever getting tired of it. I admire him, and he simply lets me.

With trembling fingers, I start unbuttoning my cardigan, one button at a time. His eyes dart to my fingers as he tracks every movement, waiting patiently. Taking a deep breath, I slide the cardigan off my shoulders, then peel off my cami, leaving myself in nothing but my lacy black bra.

Hunter's eyes darken at the sight, his chest rising and falling a little faster now.

He pushes his gray sweatpants down, stepping out of them and leaving himself in black boxer briefs that cling snugly to his hips, outlining powerful thighs, and the unmistakable shape of his cock beneath the fabric.

Oh God. Will that even fit in me?

Suddenly, I feel shy. Heat creeps up my cheeks.

Swallowing, I hook my thumbs into my skirt and slide it down my legs before quickly kicking off my socks and shoes, leaving me in just my matching lace set. It's the nicest set of undies I own. I remember buying it months ago, telling myself that one day I'd wear it for something like this. I just never imagined that day would actually come.

Hunter smiles as he takes me in. "Damn, Holly...you had all that hidden beneath those clothes?" His question is so quiet I barely catch it, like he's muttering the words more to himself than to me.

He takes two steps toward me and stops. Heat radiates from his body, close enough now that I can feel it against my skin. His scent hits me stronger this time—warm and clean, sandalwood and amber wrapped around something fresher, maybe bergamot or sage. It's the kind of smell that makes you lean in without thinking. And I do. I'm drawn to it—earthy and magnetic, edged with just enough spice to make my skin tingle.

He rests his forehead against mine as I finally gather the courage to reach out, my palm pressing to his sculpted stomach. His muscles flex beneath my touch and a low groan slips from him. In return, his fingers glide over my ribs before sliding down the curve of my waist to settle on my hips.

"We'll go slow," Hunter murmurs, his voice laced with reassurance. "We've got all the time in the world."

His lips brush over mine again—so soft and so slow that it makes me ache. Every kiss is deliberate, like he's studying me, memorizing the way I gasp when he sucks gently on my bottom lip. He trails kisses down my jaw, then lower, until his mouth finds the hollow of my throat. I arch instinctively, my body responding before my mind can catch up.

"You're shaking," he murmurs against my skin, his voice deep and silky. His hands cup my waist, grounding me. "Do you want to stop?"

He keeps asking me and I feel guilty for being so nervous. But I don't want to stop. I want him.

I shake my head, breath catching. "No. Just... don't let go."

He smiles against my lips, "Never."

Then kisses me again—deeper this time, firmer, more certain. He lifts me in his arms and carries me to his bed. It isn't rushed or clumsy. The feel of his bare skin against mine sends a rush through me; I am so wet, it's embarrassing.

He lays me down carefully, like I'm fragile, then hovers above me, searching my face, silently offering one last chance to change my mind. I don't take it. I wouldn't even consider it.

His hands explore, slow and reverent, tracing the curve of my waist, the gentle swell of my hip, the softness of my thighs. Goosebumps rise in their wake. He presses kisses to every inch of my naked skin, whispering quiet praise against me as he moves. When his mouth finds my breast through the lace of my bra, a soft, broken sound slips from my lips—one I barely recognize as my own.

He glances up at me through dark lashes, eyes burning. "You're so damn beautiful, Holly."

I pull him closer, threading my fingers in his hair, and for the first time in my life, I want to come undone. Hunter presses his forehead to mine again, breathing me in like he can't get enough.

"Still okay?" he asks, voice low and steady.

"Yes," I breathe, barely above a whisper.

His hand slides slowly between us, fingers tracing over the lace of my panties. I gasp as my hips lift instinctively, every nerve sparking to life. I've never been touched before—not like this. Not by someone who makes me feel wanted. Like I matter. Like *this* matters.

Hunter moves down my body, maddeningly slow before propping himself up on his elbows. Eyes gleaming, he gazes at me. "I've got you," he murmurs.

I blink as he hooks a finger into the waistband of my panties and gently slides them down, pressing a slow kiss to the inside of my thigh as he does. My breath stutters, the edges of the room blurring as the sensation overtakes me. I feel stripped down—bare in more ways than one.

With careful, deliberate movements, his long fingers begin to stroke and circle my clit. I gasp at the sensation. Heat floods my cheeks as I realize how responsive my body already is. So wet. So charged up. Hunter just smiles as he continues.

"You're so fucking wet, Holly."

He draws his fingers away, giving my lips a couple of strokes before pressing his mouth on them. A rasp leaves my mouth as I curl my fingers in his hair, unable to look at him.

With a flat tongue and slow intentional licks, he tastes me. I moan so loud, it surprises me. The sensation overwhelms me as he leisurely drags his tongue up and down my slit. My back arches, my fingers twisting into the sheets as he takes his time, learning what makes me tremble. Why does it feel so incredible? Is this what I've been missing out on?

When he thrusts his tongue inside of me, I combust. Juices explode—my body lights with sensation. His pace quickens as he uses his skilled mouth on me, then adds a finger back onto my clit, stroking. I lose whatever fragile control I had left. Heat coils tight against his tongue, sharper with every stroke. And I fall apart.

The release hits me suddenly, intensely—my body shuddering from an orgasm. Pleasure rushes through me in waves I've never felt before. I don't know how to hold it, how to contain it. I just feel.

My chest heaves as Hunter slowly withdraws—his lips glistening with my wetness.

"Damn, Holly... what a good girl you are."

He reaches toward the top bedside drawer for protection, that's when I notice his own hand trembling slightly.

"Are you okay?" I whisper. "Your hand... it's trembling."

He huffs out a quiet breath, almost a laugh. "Yeah. Just nervous."

The thought of this man being nervous puts a grin on my face. It makes him more human, the fact that this confident, all-star basketball player can in fact feel nerves just like the rest of us.

"You too?" I ask softly, nerves flickering back to life. Then, he pulls his boxer briefs down and kicks them away. My eyes widen. Holy shit, it's even bigger than I thought.

"Yeah," he admits, meeting my eyes as he rolls the condom on with careful focus. "It's you, Holly. I just want it to be good for you."

He settles between my thighs again, positioning himself carefully. He kisses me again, slow and deep, his lips telling me everything he doesn't say out loud. "You ready, baby? We'll go slow."

I nod.

He exhales and nudges the thick head of his cock against my entrance, pausing there. His eyes flicker downward, watching carefully, jaw tight as he begins to press forward. The stretch is immediate—big, intense, and a little painful. My breath catches, fingers tightening around his arms. It's unfamiliar, overwhelming, a sharp sensation that makes me tense as our bodies begin to join.

"Hey," he leans closer and whispers against my cheek, "look at me, okay?"

I hadn't realized my eyes had slipped shut, but I open them at once. His eyes stay locked on mine, grounding me as he eases in and out slowly, inch by inch, easing forward and then pausing whenever my breath stutters. The stretch burns at first, but only for a moment, until my body begins to adjust.

Slowly, he goes in a bit, then out, letting me grow used to the sensation. Used to him. Gradually, the feeling softens into something fuller, deeper, more consuming as my body relaxes around him.

"I've got you," he murmurs against my mouth, his voice strained as he slowly pulls out, just to the head and then slowly pushes back in. He's holding himself in check, I can feel it. "You're doing so good, Holly. Christ... you're taking me so well."

A tear slips down my cheek, and I don't fully understand why. It doesn't hurt. It isn't too much. Maybe it's the weight of the moment. Maybe it's because this feels real in a way nothing else ever has. Because I'm finally giving something I guarded so tightly—and it isn't being taken. It's being held, cherished, respected—and that realization is overwhelming.

Hunter wipes the tear away with his thumb and kisses me softly, like we've just shared something sacred. Perhaps we have.

He begins to move a little more, slow and shallow, letting me feel everything. And I do. The strong ridges of his hard cock stretch me in the most delicious of ways. The rhythm builds in tiny waves, a gentle back and forth that ignites my whole body from the inside out.

"Fuck, you're so tight, Holly," he groans—the sound reverberates from his chest as he lazily continues pushing in and out. His hands drift over my body, tracing my skin, while I press my palm to his chest and feel his heart racing beneath it.

It isn't extraneous, or loud, or fast. It's slow, euphoric as I feel every vein of him sliding in and out of me. The sensation is overwhelmingly delicious, addictive, and ours. This moment. Our first coming together. It's just Hunter and I, stripped down—raw and consumed. And for the first time, I think I understand what it really means to make love.

CHAPTER 14

Holly

I WATCH HUNTER THROUGH my laptop screen, legs tucked under me, still wrapped in the sweatshirt he left behind. It smells like him—clean, warm, a little woodsy—and I swear I can still feel his hands on my skin. The scent has faded slightly, but it lingers enough to make my stomach flip.

The arena noise blares through my speakers. The student section at the rival school is deafening. Hunter sprints across the court like a flash of navy-and-gold. He looks bigger somehow. Fiercer. There's a focus that takes over him during games—a switch that flips—and suddenly he's all instinct and precision.

I bite my lip as he muscles past a defender, his jersey stretching across his shoulder, sweat dampening the back of his neck. My thighs squeeze together before I can stop myself.

God help me. I'm officially that girl. The star basketball player's girlfriend.

At least, I hope I am.

Ever since the Jumbotron incident—since Hunter made it very clear to an entire arena that I exist—I've been getting looks. It's only been two days, but I feel them everywhere. Lingering stares from strangers who seem to recognize me from somewhere but can't quite place why. Others even approaching me and asking me questions.

"You and Hunter, huh? How'd that happen?"

"What are you to Hunter?"

"Are you guys dating?"

And then there are whispers when I walk by. Especially from other girls.

"The girl from the library?"

"How did she manage that?"

"She's probably a gold digger."

"Hoe."

I don't understand how people can be so cruel when they don't even know me. They don't know what Hunter and I are to each other, and it's all still so new that I'm not even sure how to answer the comments. All I know is that we care about each other—that what we have is this fragile, glowing little beginning—and we're still figuring it out.

I haven't told Hunter about the name-calling. I'm not sure if I will. I don't want to upset him or distract him. Not now. Not when he's hyper-focused with March Madness bracket picks coming up in a few days. Not when he's grinding to pull his Shakespeare grade up to passing, and catching up on work from the classes he missed. He already has enough on his plate.

So instead, I decide to keep my head down. Lay low. Ignore the haters. I go to class and work. Grab the occasional caramel latte at the Nest. Otherwise, I stay home. Study. Read. Honestly... I'll just stick to what I did before I met Hunter.

On my screen, Hunter scores again, pumping his fist as he sprints down the court. The camera follows him—his charisma oozing through the broadcast. God, he's so unfairly handsome. His dark hair falls across his forehead before he pushes it back, his sharp features set in fierce concentration. How did I get so lucky to catch this guy's attention?

The game ends a little after 10:45 P.M. I shut my laptop and curl into bed, snuggling up in Hunter's sweatshirt. My eyes grow heavy as I scroll mindlessly through my phone.

Just after midnight, it buzzes against my hand, lighting up the dark space and jolting me awake.

You still awake, Short-Stack?

I wasn't, but I stayed up and watched you play without falling asleep. So, I'm expecting some praise.

...such a good girl.

I don't know why that gives me all the warm fuzzies, but my nether-regions purr. I bite down on a smile as I type.

I even wore your sweatshirt for good luck.

You wore my sweatshirt??

Yep…still am.

Damn. Now I'm picturing you in just that and nothing else.

Well…you wouldn't be wrong.

You trying to kill me from three states away? Because mission accomplished.

My smile widens. Quickly, I turn on my camera and shift onto my knees, lifting my phone just enough to catch the oversized sweatshirt draped over me—bare legs tucked beneath it. I take the shot and send it before I can overthink it.

Three dots appear. Disappear. Reappear.

Then—

You're actually try to kill me. That sweatshirt's never going to be the same ever again.

You look…

Damn, Holly. You look like you belong to me.

Is that a problem?

It's the opposite of a problem. It's the kind of thing that's going to keep me up all night.

And not just because I'm imagining what's under it...

You already know what's under it...

Doesn't mean I'm not still fantasizing about it days later.

Hmm...too bad you're so far away...

Don't tease me... I might have to Uber back to campus... even if it is from three states away.

I laugh softly, shaking my head as I reread the text.

Go to sleep, Hot Shot...I'll see you soon.

Fine, but fair warning...I'm definitely dreaming of you in nothing but my jersey next.

Good night, Hunter.

Sweet dreams, baby.

I grin as I set my phone down. Now I'm a bit wired myself, thinking of Hunter... thinking of what we did. What I want to do again. The man is a walking thirst-trap, and now that I've had a taste, I want nothing more than to keep drinking.

The next day, I'm working my shift at the library. It's relatively quiet. A few students are actually studying. A few others wander in and out. Brandy arrives for her tutoring session with her athlete, some baseball player.

"Hey, Holly!" she calls as she walks in, approaching the desk. "How's the day going?"

I groan dramatically. "Slow... so darn slow."

The only upside is that I've managed to get ahead on my homework. I've already organized and returned books and re-shelved everything. I even finished a large copying order for one of the professors earlier.

Now? I'm out of tasks. Completely.

Brandy laughs. "Sounds about right. So... how's tutoring with Hunter going?"

I stare at her with a knowing smirk. She knows damn well how it's going. "Fine," I say casually. "Obviously."

"Sounds like it's going *WAY* better than fine, Holly." Her light blue eyes narrow with a familiar, mischievous sparkle. "Come on, Hols. I want deets!"

I roll my eyes, pretending to reorganize the pens at the desk.

"You *have* to give me something!" she presses. "Please tell me he's as godly underneath as he is on the outside."

I snort, before I can stop myself. "What do you think?"

Brandy groans dramatically; clenching her fists. "Ugh, I'm so jealous! You're so lucky, Hols! My athlete is just an asshole who won't even pretend to care about tutoring. It's the worst hour of my week!"

That makes me laugh—full, unrestrained.

"If anyone can handle it, it's you, Brandy," I reassure her.

She crosses her arms and shifts her weight onto one hip with a sigh. "I guess." She rolls her eyes and just as she does, a tall guy walks in. Dirty-blonde hair styled into a modern mullet, Hawks Baseball sweatshirt stretched across his broad shoulders. I assume this is her athlete. He's objectively attractive. Well-built. Athletic.

"Let's go, Lane. I don't have all day."

He doesn't even slow down as he passes her. My impression of him sours immediately. Rude.

Her face twists as she watches him stride past in tight mid-thigh shorts, athletic socks, and slides paired with the sweatshirt. I bite back a laugh at the outfit, but she just growls.

"Was waiting on you, Wells!" she calls after him, clearly irritated. Then glances back at me, seething, "Better go."

She stalks after the jock, shoulders stiff.

"Oof." I murmur to myself, a tsk-tsk escaping my mouth as I shake my head watching them disappear.

A deep voice pulls my attention back to the desk.

"Hey, Short-Stack." Hunter leans casually against the reception counter, an easy smile spreading across his face as his eyes sweep over me.

"Hey," I gasp, unable to hide my excitement. "You just get back?" I start to stand, and he's already rounding the side of the desk to meet me.

"Yeah, not too long ago," he says. "You have a minute?"

I glance around the library before answering.

"I probably have a few to spare," I admit quietly.

"Cool." Hunter grabs my hand. "Come with me."

He starts pulling me toward the stacks. I frown slightly as we head deeper into the library, passing the study room where Brandy and her athlete are clearly bickering behind the glass.

"Is everything okay?" I ask, breathless, trying to keep up as he moves at a determined pace.

He doesn't answer. He just keeps walking, guiding me farther into the quieter, dimmer part of the library where the shelves feel taller and the air feels heavier. We pass our usual tutoring room without stopping. For every step he takes, I feel like I'm taking three.

His hand firmly holds onto mine as he guides me, sending a thrill through me. I look around, to make sure no one's nearby. There isn't.

"Hunter," I whisper, half-confused, half-exhilarated. "Where are you taking me?"

Once we're well out of earshot, he pulls me into a narrow row of outdated encyclopedias—thick leather-bound volumes no one has touched in years—and presses me gently but firmly back against the shelves, boxing me in.

My heart slams against my chest as I look up into his dark, hungry eyes.

And then, his mouth is on mine.

Almost instantly, I melt in his arms as he wraps them around me. His hands move over me frantically and the kiss is deep—consuming, like he's trying to make up for lost time.

"Fuck, I missed you," he breathes against my mouth before trailing kisses down my neck. "All I've been thinking about is that naughty photo you sent me."

It wasn't even naughty, but seeing what I do to him is a huge turn on. His lips against my heated skin make me shiver. His fingers thread through my hair as he presses closer, and a soft moan slips from me. I can feel what I do to him, how much he missed me, how much he wants me. It's intoxicating.

I instantly regret wearing chinos today, wishing I'd chosen a skirt instead, eager for his fingers to caress my bare skin.

He cups my breast, kneading gently, while I slide my hands beneath his t-shirt, exploring all the divots of his muscles. His skin flexes beneath my touch and it elicits a feral want within me.

"I missed you too." I whisper as he continues kissing me, his cologne clouding my senses and making everything feel hazy.

"I fucking need you, Holly."

Before I fully register it, he's unbuttoning my chinos, slipping his hand inside my pants. When his fingers slide beneath the lace of my panties, he strokes my clit and my body seizes.

"Hunter," I whisper-moan. "You're going to get me in trouble."

My head rolls back as his fingers explore my folds, slickness oozing.

"Maybe I want you to get in trouble," he murmurs against my ear. "Maybe I want to see that naughty librarian side of you."

A fresh wave of heat floods through me.

Oh God. This man...

When he eases a finger inside me, my body arches instinctively. My knees wobble, and he braces me with his free arm. I grab him tighter and just when I get used to it a bit, he pushes a second finger into my core. "Ah!" A startled moan escapes.

"Shhh," he coos. "I don't want anyone to hear those sounds but me."

I clutch at his hair as he moves his fingers in and out with steady confidence, his mouth returning to my neck, sucking my skin between his lips. The sensation builds quickly—warm and pulsing. My core flutters as he continues pushing and pulling, rubbing me in a controlled rhythm. The pressure grows, cresting steadily, until my core throbs and tightens around him, squeezing his fingers tight. He slows slightly, drawing out the sensation, letting it hover just at the edge.

"Come for me, Holly," Hunter commands. "Be the good girl I know you are, and let me feel you come on my fingers."

His words undo me.

My body tightens, every muscle drawing taut before my orgasm breaks loose and crashes through me. My heart pounds wildly in my chest as I cling to him, the waves rolling until I can barely stand. Hunter's hand remains steady inside my pants while I breathe hard against his shoulder, trembling from the inside out.

I don't know how long we stay like that, frozen within that moment of bliss, but it's endless and electric. I don't want to move.

Hunter keeps a firm hold on me as I come down, my shaky legs beginning to steady beneath me. Gentle kisses brush along my jaw as my breathing evens out. When I can finally stand on my own, he removes his hand, brings his fingers to his mouth, sucking my juices clean off them. The sight is brazen and intimate, yet satisfying in a way I can't explain. Heat rushes into my face. The dark amusement on his face only makes it worse.

I've no idea how long I've been gone from the front desk, but right now, I can't seem to care.

We just did that... in the library.

"I just needed a taste of you, baby," he murmurs, his voice hoarse. "God, you consume my every thought."

There's almost something tortured in the way he says it, and a twinge of uncertainty stirs inside me. I've never had this effect on anyone before. I don't know how to hold that. How to give that back.

I nod my head, still catching my breath, unsure what to say. Hunter cups my face gently, guiding my gaze back to him. "Hey. You are so beautiful, Holly. And that was only the tiniest taste of what I want from you."

He kisses me again—deep but slower this time—before slowly pulling away.

A haze of wanton lust lingers over me, my body still buzzing as a flush spreads across my cheeks.

He gives me a mischievous smirk. "Maybe later we can continue this?"

I huff a breath, a small smile tugging at my lips. "Sure," I manage. "I think I'd like that."

He hums in approval and presses one last chaste kiss onto my mouth.

"I'll see you later, baby."

Hunter winks at me before leaving me a completely shattered, turned-on mess... it's glorious.

CHAPTER 15

Holly

IT'S THE DAY OF the NCAA March Madness bracket reveal, and the entire campus feels charged with anticipation. Hunter told me that he and the team were having a private viewing party in their locker room, hoping for two things: first, that they make the tournament. And second, that they secure a decent seed. Significant others weren't allowed at the viewing, but he did invite me to the party at Whitmore House afterward—the Beta Rho Chi fraternity house, which he's a member of.

I said yes. But now, I'm having second thoughts.

Over the past week, Hunter and I have been spotted together more and more, drawing attention almost everywhere we go. He's used to this. I'm not.

As I stand in front of my closet, rifling through hangers and discarded outfits, my nerves grow by the minute. I have no idea what to wear to a frat party. I've never actually been to one before. Brandy invited me to her sorority party once, and I politely declined. I've walked past plenty. Heard the music.

Seen the crowds. But I've never attended one. Especially not as the date of the school's star basketball player.

My laptop hums in the background with the NCAA March Madness Bracket show streaming live. Every few minutes, I glance over to see if they've started announcing teams yet. But for the past hour, the sportscasters have only been rambling on all speculation and their opinions.

It's all gibberish to me. I still don't understand most of the technical nuances of the game, though I've picked up more over the past few weeks from watching Hunter play and spending time around him.

The last home game, I had to work, so I couldn't attend. But the library was nearly empty, which meant I was able to stream it quietly on ESPN+ from my phone.

Discreetly, of course.

Hunter always looks good on the court. He just does. But during the last game, there was a moment when he seemed winded—pale, even. The coach pulled him for a few minutes, and from what I could see, he recovered well enough to go back in.

When I asked Hunter about it later that evening, he shrugged it off. Said it was just mid-game fatigue, which, sounded believable. I can tell basketball is physically demanding—I can see that much—but I don't personally understand the toll it takes on the body. I've never played a competitive sport like that.

One evening when Hunter had an off night, we curled up in his dorm room and he put on one of their rival's games. As we watched, he explained some of the basketball stuff. He told me about the different positions of players, what they did, what different fouls were, and why sometimes there were three free throws instead of two.

I liked listening to him talk about something he loves. It's evident that basketball lives inside him, lives within his soul. He lights up when he talks about it, charisma slipping into every word. I must have been staring at him with a ridiculous smile, because when he caught me, he teased me about it. And, that naturally turned into… something else, something much more sensual and delicious.

From my laptop, theme music swells and the sportscaster's voice booms through my room.

"…And welcome back to ESPN's exclusive coverage of Selection Sunday! We're moments away from revealing this year's official NCAA March Madness Bracket. Sixty-eight teams. One champion. And it all starts now."

I step closer to the laptop, cardigan still clutched in my hands as bright graphics flash across the screen: **March Madness 2025 – Official Bracket Reveal**.

"…Let's begin with the South Region. Grabbing the number one seed, the University of Alabama! No surprise there. They've had a dominant season."

I tune out of the chatter for a moment and slide the cardigan back into my closet, searching instead for another top.

"Next up, the eight-versus-nine seed match up: Kansas State will face off against Oregon..."

I finally settle on a white babydoll crop top that I'd completely forgotten about and pair it with a navy pleated skirt—mostly because I know how much Hunter likes them. And because it matches our school colors.

Once dressed, I wander back to my laptop and notice they've moved quickly through the bracket reveals. Graphics swirl across the screen as each match up is announced.

"And sliding into that coveted number three seed in the East Region... make some noise for Westbridge State University! The Hawks are in!"

The broadcast cuts to a live feed of the team's locker room. The players erupt into celebration, and right at the center of it all is Hunter. I cheer at my screen, unable to stop myself. He's grinning ear to ear, hugging his teammates as confetti from party poppers rain down around them. The whole room is bouncing with energy.

"Led by standout senior center Hunter Jace, the Hawks have been on a tear this season, boasting a massive 27-4 record. They'll face off against Montana in the first round."

A rush of pride overcomes me. That's my man.

I can't stop smiling as I watch him shake hands with the coaches, their hands clapping his shoulders in congratulations. He's worked so hard for this and he looks proud. When the broadcast returns to the rest of the bracket coverage, I step away to finish getting ready. It won't be long before I need to head to the party.

I'm standing outside a grand colonial-style house that looks like something pulled from an old southern campus brochure—red brick, black shutters, towering white columns trying just a little too hard to project prestige. I hesitate on the sidewalk, fiddling with my wristlet and wondering, not for the first time tonight, what the hell I'm doing here.

I'm not a frat party girl.

But this isn't just any frat party. This is Hunter's frat party. The one they're throwing to celebrate snagging a three seed in the tournament. *The NCAA March Madness* tournament. The one he invited me to, saying he'd like me to meet his friends, and of course, teammates.

I take a steady breath and step forward, the bass from inside vibrating faintly through the soles of my shoes as I push through the large double doors.

Inside, the air is thick with heat, cologne, beer, and the heavy thump of a remix I can't name. The hardwood floors are already sticky, and the house is packed with people I don't know—most clutching red Solo cups like accessories.

I weave through the crowd toward what looks like the main living room. Someone has scrawled the full March Madness bracket across a giant whiteboard, with Westbridge State circled boldly in blue marker.

My eyes scan the room, searching for Hunter, but I don't see him anywhere. My heart races as I begin to feel a little claustrophobic in a space filled with strangers.

There are a lot of girls here—tiny dresses, towering heels, glossy hair. Cheerleaders, maybe. I'm not entirely sure.

I feel very different from them. A few of them glance my way, then lean toward each other whispering.

"*Is that her*?" The question carries through the crowd. I keep walking, pretending not to hear, trying to find Hunter.

"I think so... yeesh. Kind of mousy, isn't she?"

I roll my eyes and ignore it. Or at least, try to.

When I reach the kitchen, it's just as crowded—at least a dozen people squeezed around the island—but Hunter isn't there either. My shoulders slump slightly as I stand there, feeling out of place in a house I'm not familiar with, surrounded by people who clearly know each other.

"Hey! You're Jace's girl, yeah?"

The words were loud and clear, aimed straight at me. I shudder a little as I turn and see a tall, dark guy. I recognize him from the court.

"Yes," I squeak out.

He flashes a wide, warm smile and extends his hand. "Hunter's told me a lot about you. I'm Jalen Carter. Junior Power Forward."

Up close, his brown eyes are warm, and his hair is buzzed short with a sharp design shaved into the sides. I remember noticing it during games.

"Nice to meet you. I'm Holly."

He steps beside me and offers a red Solo cup.

"What's in it?" I ask cautiously.

Jalen laughs as he hands it to me. "Crappy keg beer of some kind."

I wrinkle my nose but accept it anyway. "Thanks?"

"No problem."

I glance around again. "So... have you seen Hunter?"

"Don't worry," Jalen says easily. "I'll hang with you until he gets here. He's the man of the hour. Probably got stuck doing an interview or something back at the arena."

That makes sense.

"So, tell me," he continues, leaning against the counter, "how'd you two meet?"

I raise a brow and take the smallest possible sip of the beer. It's gross—flat and watery—I try not to gag as I force it down my throat. I set the cup down on the counter with no intention of picking it back up. "At the library," I admit.

Jalen laughs—a full, booming sound that makes me smile.

"Well, yeah, the library part was obvious. But *how*? How did a cute girl like you snag a dumb shit like Hunter?"

I burst out laughing. "A dumb shit? I mean... he's a little smarter than he leads on, I think."

Jalen studies me for a moment, his expression shifting. His eyes narrow slightly as he really looks at me. "I can see it," he says at last.

"See what?"

"Why he likes you." A mischievous grin spreads across his dapper face. "He's kind of crazy about you."

My cheeks flush as I glance down at my feet.

"Thanks... I think," I mumble with a soft laugh.

Just then, one of the girls from the living room strides into the kitchen. As she passes, she slams her shoulder into mine, hard, and shoots me a malicious glare.

"Whoops. Sorry," she says dryly, flipping her long blonde hair over her shoulder. I freeze, unsure how to respond.

"Hey, cool it, Tammie-Lee." Jalen says sharply. She pivots, fixing him with striking green eyes.

"What? You fucking her too?" she snaps as she fills her cup from the keg. I go rigid.

"Absolutely not," Jalen fires back. "Don't be a bitch just 'cause you don't have Hunter's attention."

Tammie-Lee glares at him for a beat longer before brushing past us. "Fuck you, J," she mutters as she exits the kitchen.

The noise of the party rushes back in once she's gone, but my hands are trembling at my sides. Self-doubt creeps in. Maybe I shouldn't be here. Maybe I was right. I don't belong here.

"Don't listen to her, Holly," Jalen says gently. "She's just jealous. She's been eyeing Hunter for like eight months." He places a warm, large hand over mine, grounding me. "You're exactly where you're supposed to be."

I try to smile, but it doesn't quite stick. "Thanks," I mumble.

A sudden roar erupts from the other room—cheers and whistles cutting through the music.

"Guess the All-Star finally showed up," Jalen jokes, nodding toward the noise as he heads that way. He gestures for me to follow.

I do, though my thoughts are still tangled.

I see Hunter before he sees me.

He's standing in the middle of the room, hair pushed back from his forehead, flashing that bright smile. He's wearing a Westbridge State Basketball t-shirt and dark jeans that fit just right, sneakers clean and bright under the lights.

He looks effortless. Confident.

All-American in the most unfair way.

My mouth goes dry.

People crowd around him, clapping his back, pulling him into half-hugs, offering high-fives and fist bumps. He accepts it all easily.

Out of the corner of my eye, I spot Tammie-Lee striding over toward him. She throws her arms around him, pressing herself in close. He returns the hug stiffly, polite but distant, and then gently distances himself. His gaze lifts, scanning the room. A quiet hope blooms in my chest. Maybe he's searching for me.

Then his eyes find mine. And everything else fades.

CHAPTER 16

Holly

HUNTER IGNORES EVERYTHING AND everyone as he darts toward me, his eyes locked and determined. I catch myself biting my lower lip as he reaches me and pulls me into a tight bear hug, lifting me clean off my feet. I squeal, but he cuts the sound off with a deep, passionate kiss.

The room erupts into loud "oohs" and cheers, and my face flushes as he finally pulls back flashing that signature megawatt smile.

"Hey, baby," he whispers in my ear before slowly sliding me down the length of his body until my feet touch the floor again.

"Hey," I say, a little breathless. "Congratulations, Hot-Shot. You made it."

He laughs softly, running a hand through his hair. "Yeah... we made it." He leans down as kisses me again—this one slower, softer, almost reverent.

"Alright, alright," Jalen interrupts, stepping up and giving Hunter a light punch to the arm. "Quit sucking face. You left your girl hanging. I almost stole her away while you were gone." He winks at me, and I can't help but giggle.

"Is that so?" Hunter shoots him a look before glancing down at me with a raised brow.

"More like he rescued me from the sea of strangers," I admit.

Hunter frowns slightly before pulling me closer to his side. "Sorry. I got stuck doing interviews. Then ESPN called for a phone segment. I didn't plan on staying as long as I did."

I nod. "I get it. It's a big moment for you guys."

"Come on," Jalen says, throwing an arm around Hunter's shoulders. "Let's get the man of the hour a drink."

The three of us head back into the kitchen.

The same group of girls from earlier are clustered near the counter, drinks in hand, heads bent together. As we walk in, I feel their eyes on me again. Hunter doesn't seem to notice. But Jalen does. Our eyes meet briefly, and I know he saw it too.

Grabbing a red Solo cup, Hunter walks to the keg to pour a beer, but Tammie-Lee and her little circle shift in front of it, blocking his way like a barricade. She plants herself there as if he needs permission to pass.

"Excuse me, Tam," Hunter says evenly.

She doesn't budge. Instead, she crosses her arms, pushing her chest up, and tilts her head so her bleached hair slips over to one shoulder. A slow, suggestive smile curves her lips.

"Not until you kiss me like you kissed her." She flicks her gaze in my direction.

His brows lower instantly. His entire demeanor changes. "Why the hell would I do that?"

"Oh," she replies sweetly, though there's nothing sweet about it, "so you're not giving kisses like that to everyone anymore? You used to. Pretty sure you enjoyed more than one girl at a time."

Hunter's shoulders go rigid. His jaw tightens, nostrils flaring slightly. The low sound that escapes him is close to a growl. "Piss off, Tammie-Lee. Don't be a bitch."

Tammie-Lee shakes, yet standing taller than before. "A bitch? Really, Hunter? Like, what the fuck. You were all over me like a month ago, and now this little mouse shows up from nowhere and suddenly you're acting brand new? I mean, who the fuck is this bitch?"

Hunter sets his empty cup down harder than necessary on the counter and steps closer to her, eyes blazing. "She is none of your business, Tammie-Lee. And you're delusional if you thought we were together 'like a month ago'." He makes air quotes. "It's been six months. I'm not interested. Holly is my girlfriend, so shut the fuck up and back off."

My heart flutters. Girlfriend.

It's the first time he's called me that. I like the way it sounds—warm and certain—yet the feeling quickly fades as I watch Tammie-Lee's face twist.

Her eyes flash with anger, her nose wrinkling in open disgust. "Hunter Jace, you're the biggest fucking player out there... and not in a good way. When you get bored of her, you know where to find me."

She storms past us, slamming into my shoulder harder than before. I wince, instinctively grabbing the spot as her friends trail after her, shooting daggers in my direction.

Hunter is at my side instantly, his hand warm against my shoulder. "Shit. Is this what you were dealing with before I got here?"

Jalen and I exchange a brief look.

Hunter exhales sharply. "Come on, Holly. Let's go."

"But it's your party—" I stutter, but he's already taking my hand, guiding me firmly through the crowded living room and out the front doors.

The cool night air hits me like a reset button. The sudden shift from pounding music to the soft hum of crickets and distant traffic makes my head spin. I inhale deeply, feeling like I can finally breathe.

Hunter slams the doors shut behind us and turns to face me, frustration written all over his face. "I don't care if it's my party, but it's really not. It's the team's. The frats. But I'm not going to stand there while you get harassed by stupid bimbo basketball groupies." He grips my upper arms gently but firmly, making sure I'm looking at him. "You mean more to me than some party. I'm sorry I wasn't here sooner to protect you from it."

"Hunter..." I drawl. "Maybe, I don't belong in your world."

The words hang between us. The air thickens.

"What?" His entire body stiffens. "What are you talking about?"

"Hunter, think about it," I press softly. "You're a celebrity on this campus. Even in the city. And me? I'm nobody. I'm nothing. I'm not special, Hunter. And since I've been hanging out with you, I've been whispered about, stared at, called names I've never been called before."

"What?" he demands again, anger simmering beneath the word. "Why didn't you tell me?"

"You can't control gossip," I say quietly. "You can't stop jealous girls who wish they were in my place. But it's a lot for me. The spotlight, the attention, I'm not used to it. I'm not used to being stared at like I'm some novelty or some sort of lucky charm on your belt."

Hunter flinches, like the words physically hit him. "Holly... what are you saying? That you don't want to be with me?"

"That's not what I'm saying..." I rush out, gesturing helplessly around us. "It's the scrutiny. I feel like I'm constantly being examined, judged. Like I'm not what people expect you to be with. I don't live up to their expectations."

He lets out a sharp breath. "Who cares about their expectations? You live up to mine—that's all that should matter. Don't extinguish the fire because you can't handle the heat. We have something special. Come on, Short-Stack, you're stronger than this. Braver."

"I'm not used to this!" I snap, my voice rising despite myself. "I don't know how to handle it. I'm not like you, Hunter. I'm not charismatic. I'm not charming. I'm quiet. I like blending in." My hands clench at my sides, chest rising and falling too fast.

He goes still as takes me in.

The furrow in his brow relaxes and he exhales slowly before reaching for my hand.

"You're right, Holly," he says softly. "You're not like me."

His thumb caresses the top of my hand. A subtle smile sprawls across his lips. When his eyes meet mine, they're intense, captivating, yet sincere.

"You're better," he continues. "You're smart and clever. Funny and sassy. You're sweet without even trying to be. And damn it, Holly, you are so beautiful, inside and out."

His grip tightens slightly.

"I'm crazy about you. Even though it's only been a few weeks, you've enthralled me from the moment we bumped into each other. I saw you and those gorgeous honey-colored eyes and I was done before I even knew your name."

My breath stutters as I roll my eyes, trying to blink back the sudden sting of tears. Hunter gently grips my chin, lifting my face so I have no choice but to look at him.

"So don't quit on us, Holly," he says firmly. "Don't give up on us just because of some petty girls. They don't have me. They don't know me. You do." His voice drops, steadier now. "You have me. All of me.

And damn it, I will fight for it, baby. I will fight, and I'm not letting you go without one."

My breath catches again—but this time it's different. Not disbelief. Something deeper. Warmer. Terrifying in its honesty.

Hunter's hold on my chin softens, his thumb brushing slowly along my jaw like he's committing it to memory. I search his face, for a crack, a flinch, anything that suggests he doesn't mean what he's saying.

But all I see is truth. Certainty.

All I feel is him choosing me.

And for the first time since I set foot into this world of roaring crowds and glossy cheerleaders, I don't feel like I'm trespassing.

I feel like I belong.

Like he's holding the door open to his heart—and I'm standing right at the threshold.

I blink up at him, my throat tight. "I don't know what to say," I whisper honestly. There are thousands of thoughts swirling in my mind, but none of them make it past the lump in my throat.

His brows knit together slightly, like he's bracing himself.

But I don't step back.

Instead, I lean just barely into his touch.

"I don't want to lose you either," I admit, my voice so quiet it seems like a whisper in the early spring breeze. And that's all I've got. For now.

His hand slips from my face and grabs my hand instead—gentle, grounding. He doesn't speak. Doesn't push.

He just starts walking, close enough that our arms brush. Ever so quiet. Like he's terrified the spell will break if he says or does anything else.

My heart pounds. Thunders in my chest. Not with fear, but with certainty. Because I know where this is heading. And this time, I'm not pulling away.

CHAPTER 17

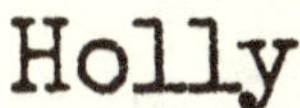

Holly

THE DOOR CLICKS SHUT behind us. Soft. Final.

Neither of us speak.

Hunter's room is dim, lit only by the faint glow of his desk lamp casting shadows across the floor. He still hasn't let go of my hand.

Instead, he turns toward me slowly, like he's afraid he might scare me off if he moves too fast. But I don't flinch. I won't run. His fingers lift to my face again, brushing beneath my cheekbones before curling gently under my chin. His touch is careful, steady.

"You really staying?" He asks, his voice thick with raw emotion. "You going to fight for us?"

I nod, barely. "I'm here," I whisper.

That's all it takes.

His mouth finds mine in a heartbeat. No teasing this time, no gentle restraint. Just heat and hunger and possessive hands that declare I'm his and he is mine. He guides me deeper into the room, until the backs of my knees hit the bed.

His hands are everywhere. On my hips, my waist, sliding up my babydoll crop top. My breath catches as his thumb traces the edge of my bra. My pulse jumps with the sensation, but I'm lost in him as he possesses me.

And then he pauses. His fingers brush against the side of my glasses. He leans in, lips ghosting over mine. "Can I?" he asks, breathless.

"Yes," I breathe.

He slides them off with surprising care and sets them on his desk, deliberate and gentle. The moment they're gone, his restraint unravels. His hands tangle into my hair, his mouth back on mine and his control completely unhinged. I fist his shirt in my hands, holding on as he presses closer. I gasp into his mouth, and he deepens the kiss in response. One hand slides down to my thigh, firm and possessive, lifting it slightly against his hip.

"Have I told you," he murmurs against my lips, his voice rough with want, "how fucking sexy you look in this outfit, Holly?"

With a gentle shove, I fall back onto the bed, a surprised breath leaving me.

"No," I answer. Hunter grins down at me, something dark and primal flashing in his eyes, as he crawls over me. The mattress dips beneath his weight, and when he settles above me, I grab the hem of his shirt and pull it over his head in one clean yank.

Holy hell, he's unreal.

His chest rises and falls steadily, his jaw tight as his gaze locks onto mine like I'm the center of his entire world. Perhaps I am in this moment. It's intoxicating—intimidating even—being looked at like that. Desired like that.

I swallow and let my hand glide slowly over his stomach, tracing the defined lines of his abs. His muscles flex. There's a faint dusting of hair across his chest, and I trail my finger down from his chest to his belly button, then down his happy trail—following the line of dark hair.

"Fuck," he hisses sliding his hand higher along my inner thigh. "You drive me insane, Holly. Every time you walk into a room. Every time you wear one of these tiny skirts." His fingers tighten slightly at my leg. "Christ, look at you… like a snack all wrapped up for me to devour."

His mouth finds my neck this time, as he plants wet kisses on my skin, his tongue hungry—possessive. No hesitation. No nerves. Just raw need. His hand squeezes around my leg and it sends a jolt of pleasure straight between my thighs. I tangle my fingers in his hair, my breath catching as he drags his lips down my bare shoulder and across my collarbone. His palm spreads over my bare stomach where my top has ridden up.

"This needs to fucking go," he chuckles, as he lifts my babydoll shirt and pulls it up and over my head. Unwrapping his little snack.

Cool air brushes my heated skin, and goosebumps rise instantly. His gaze drops to my breasts almost instantly. My nipples peak through the lining of my bra and Hunter's eyes instantly fixate on them. He pulls the cup down, revealing my small breasts. Leaning down, he immediately starts licking and sucking—his tongue sending sparks to my soul. My back arches instinctively, fingers threading through his hair as the sensation ripples through me.

The sound that leaves my mouth seems to snap something inside him. He goes feral. His hands move over me with new urgency. Rough, reverent, desperate. My top is gone, my skirt's hiked up. And when he grinds against me, I feel him—hard, undeniably so, pressed right where I'm already aching.

He doesn't fumble as he reaches down, unzipping those jeans, sliding them down just a bit before freeing himself from his boxer briefs. Seeing how big he is makes my eyes go wide. I've seen it before, yet it's still a surprise. A pleasantly delicious one.

"I want to feel you raw, Holly," his breath is ragged, like what he's asking is scandalous. His need is unhinged and his entire body vibrates against me. "Tell me it's okay."

The intensity in his expression makes my pulse jump. The understanding of his desire runs through me. I nod first, then find my voice. "Yeah… I'm on birth control."

He exhales slowly, tension easing just a fraction as he slides my panties down my legs. His fingers leaving a trail of goosebumps.

His hands slide back up my legs, he pauses near my thigh. His gaze fixates on the slickness in between them, as his fingers begin to play with my arousal.

He traces them along the folds and into the pool of wetness in a slow rhythm, sending toe-curling sensations down my spine.

Then, in a slow sensual motion, he uses my arousal to wet the head of his dick. My eyes meet his hooded ones as he gazes down at me, like he's won the lottery.

My mouth goes dry as he settles between me. The anticipation feels torturous. When I feel the head of him press at my entrance, I hold my breath. Hunter's eyes darken making him look like a dark God.

"Breathe, baby." It's the only warning I get. He thrusts all the way into me, filling me in one deep stroke. A broken cry tears from my throat, loud and unholy, echoing against the dorm room walls. My eyes squeeze shut as I try to process the fullness of him. It's overwhelming as my pussy stretches to accommodate him.

He just stays there, deep inside me, without moving, allowing my body to stretch. I can barely comprehend how my body can take all of him. It feels impossible.

Still joined, he shifts and wraps his arms around me, lifting me upright until I'm straddling him. The change of position pulls another gasp from me, tears pricking at my eyes from the intensity. My hands brace against his shoulders as I tremble.

"Shh, baby, it's okay," Hunter wipes the tears. "You're doing so well. Just keep breathing, Hols. I'm gonna start moving you, okay? Put your arms around my neck."

I obey his command allowing him full control, trusting him completely.

With one hand, he reaches behind me and unhooks my bra, sliding the straps sensually off my shoulders, pressing slow kisses to my skin as they fall. He tosses my bra off the bed and adjusts his legs, widening just a bit for a better angle. The shift makes my insides clench, and a soft moan slips from my mouth.

Hunter presses his lips to mine, kissing me softly, just once. "Here we go, baby," he whispers.

His hands slide beneath my hips, fingers sprawling wide as he lifts to guide me, setting the pace. It's slow at first, just enough for me to feel every long, delicious drag of him inside me. My eyes flutter as my head lulls back, the sensation consuming me whole.

His grip tightens and his hips begin to move in tandem with mine, thrusting up as he guides me down. Every time our bodies meet, I feel it so deep it steals the air from my lungs. I hiss through my teeth, while he grits his. He's so deep within me—my insides squeeze and adjust.

"God, Holly," he groans against my skin, voice rough with restraint. "You feel... so damn perfect. You take me so well. Such a good girl."

Each roll of his hips is controlled, deliberate. When I force my eyes open, he's watching me—his dark gaze locked onto mine like he's memorizing every expression. And when my head tips back again, he buries his mouth in my neck, biting down softly, coaxing a moan from deep in my throat.

"Yeah, baby. Just like that," he growls. "Squeeze my cock, good and tight."

His hands slide lower, gripping the curve of my ass with bruising pressure as he begins to move me faster, lifting and dropping me with more force, more need. His rhythm turns rough, relentless. The wet sound of our bodies echo within the walls of the room.

My fingers claw into his shoulders, anchoring myself to him as his hips slam into me. Every thrust pulls a gasp from my throat. Every moan grows louder, more primal.

"Fuck, Holly. You're so tight," his voice is strained. His breath turns uneven against my collarbone. "I don't think I can hold back."

"Don't," I pant, meeting his rhythm as best I can, barely holding on as my body trembles around him. "Don't hold back, Hunter."

He grabs the back of my neck, pulling me into a fierce kiss that's all teeth and tongue and suddenly everything shifts. Hunter flips us so I'm on my back and he's over me, thrusting deeper, harder, driving into me like he owns me.

I cry out, but it's not pain, it's ecstasy as my core spasms, clenching Hunter's cock inside me. He squeezes my breasts, pushing them together, teasing my nipples. "God, you're so fucking beautiful, Holly. I'm the luckiest guy in the world." He says as he pounds into me.

He's so hard and I don't know how much more I can take. His thrusting becomes short, fast and through gritted teeth he growls, "my sweet, delicious, fucking baby girl."

With one final push, he throbs inside me and the dam within me bursts with an audible cry of pleasure. My body tenses, riding the waves of pleasure before every muscle within me relaxes. It's long and drawn out as my body shakes around him. Hunter follows right after as a hoarse groan leaves his lips.

It's the sexiest sound I've ever heard.

Then, the room is filled with nothing but our heavy, ragged breaths. We stay like that for a while, still tangled together... letting our heartbeats settle.

I'm exhausted, worn out, sore, and it's beyond ecstatic. We're panting in harmony, our bodies slick with sweat. The heat of my skin begins to cool when my eyes meet with Hunter's. He's looking down at me with a satisfied grin sprawled on his face.

Eventually, he slowly pulls out, the sensation odd as he leaves me empty.

He shifts and stretches beside me, pulling me close against his bare body. And as sleep starts to pull at me, wrapped in his arms, I realize I'm safe.

CHAPTER 18

Hunter

HOLLY FALLS ASLEEP IN my arms, and I can't stop looking at her. She did so damn good tonight. My chest swells just thinking about it. The way she held herself together. The way she walked into that party, into that chaos, into my world...and stayed. She didn't crumble.

Her creamy skin feels warm against mine, soft as velvet. I press my face into her neck, breathing in that faint vanilla scent mixed with our sweat. She doesn't see herself the way I do. She doesn't think she's beautiful. Or brave. Or strong.

But she is. God, she is.

She has no idea how powerful she is just by being exactly who she is.

The thought of Tammie-Lee and the rest of those cheerleaders makes my jaw tighten again. The way they cornered her. The way they made her feel. It wasn't right. None of it was.

How long has she been dealing with that? Since we started dating?

I'm grateful Jalen stepped in. At least she wasn't completely alone. But I should've been there. I should've been the one defending her, protecting her. Bunch of basketball bimbos.

I should've met her at the arena and walked into that party with her. Why didn't I think of it earlier? Instead, I sent her to the wolves.

The thought sits heavy in my chest.

But I'll fix it. If she'll let me.

A soft sigh slips from her lips as she shifts in her sleep, curling closer to me. Instantly, the anger drains out of my body. My hand smooths over her back, slow and protective, tracing lazy patterns against her skin.

I don't know how I fell so hard, so fast for Holly Lange. But I did.

The moment we collided, those hazel-green eyes wide behind her round glasses, locked me into them. I didn't know it then, but something shifted. And then fate, or luck, or whatever cosmic force runs this world, made her my tutor. I believe in luck. And if it was divine intervention? Then, I'll gladly drop to my knees and thank whatever god decided I deserved her.

Her bare chest rises and falls slowly against mine, and I can't help but stare at her pert breasts and those dusty-rose colored nipples. She's still in that tiny pleated skirt—the one that absolutely undid me. Careful not to wake her, I ease the fabric down her legs so she can sleep comfortably. She barely stirs. I pull the comforter up around us, tucking it around her shoulders.

A strand of hair falls across her face. I brush it back softly, studying the peaceful flush of her cheeks, the slight swell of her lips from the way I attacked them.

Even asleep, she pulls at something deep inside me.

The desire is so bad, it actually aches. My cock hasn't quite caught up to the fact that she needs rest. We both do.

I'm still riding the high from tonight. My mind's restless from everything. The party, the argument, and then *this*. This moment of pure bliss with this wonderful woman in my arms.

But she needs sleep. I tighten my arm around her waist, allowing all of her to permeate my senses. In a few days, I'll be leaving for New York. March Madness. The biggest stretch of the season. I'm going to miss her. Part of me wants to ask her to come. To be there. But I won't.

She has classes. A life. Goals that don't revolve around me or a basketball court. It wouldn't be fair to her.

Her hand shifts in her sleep, settling against my chest. It's so tiny compared to mine, but the warmth of it quiets the restless edge inside me.

I'm content in this moment. I wish we could freeze it—Holly, curled into my arms, warm and safe, like the outside world doesn't exist.

I press a soft kiss to the top of her head.

For now, I just stay here. Watching her breathe. Letting the quiet settle into my bones. Bask in this lazy, still moment with the girl I love.

It's my March Madness debut. No pressure—just the biggest stage of my life so far.

I sit in the locker room at Madison Square Garden. Madison. Fucking. Square. Garden.

The name alone buzzes in my chest like live electricity. The air smells like new sneakers and floor polish. My jersey's already damp—not from sweat, but adrenaline.

How the hell did I get here?

We landed in New York two days ago, and it's been non-stop. Team picture in Times Square. Flashing billboards. Blaring horns. A rush of tourists and street performers. And that weird hotdog smell that clings to your clothes no matter how far you walk. It's incredible.

We had a few hours to explore, so I played tourist. I even bought a cheesy "I NY" t-shirt for Holly. She'll roll her eyes when she'll see it—pretend she hates it—but she'll keep it. I know she will.

I asked her to come, of course. She couldn't swing it. School, work, life.

I get it.

Still, it doesn't stop me from wishing she were here—standing next to me, fingers weaved through mine, looking up at the skyline.

Yesterday was all business: practice, drills, press conferences, photo-shoots. Posing for pictures I'll probably never see. Every minute packed. Every second ticking closer to now.

The locker room door creaks open, snapping me back.

Coach McGraw's voice cuts through the haze. "Alright, gather 'round. Listen up!"

We circle in. The room hums with nervous energy—tape ripping, sneakers squeaking against tile, water bottles snapping shut. Then silence.

Coach scans us one by one. "This isn't just a game. This is your moment. Madison Square Garden doesn't make legends, you do. Every cut, every pass, every rebound—you've been training for this your whole damn life." His voice sharpens. "You've trusted each other all season. Now, do it again. Leave everything on that floor. No regrets. You hear me?"

"Yes, Coach!" we shout back.

"Let 'em know who Westbridge is. Let 'em know who you are, who *we* are. We are the Westbridge Hawks..." He thrusts his hand into the center. We stack ours on top. "And we've come to fly!"

"Fly, Hawks!"

"Go Hawks!"

Coach throws our hands up, and the tunnel ahead glows bright.

My pulse pounds.
Showtime.

CHAPTER 19

Holly

I'm fully settled in—bowl of popcorn within reach, fleece blanket tucked around my legs, laptop balanced carefully on my thighs—as I prepare to watch the first round of March Madness from my dorm room.

Hunter is already on the screen, warming up just minutes before tip-off. Butterflies swarm in my stomach for him. I can only imagine what his nerves must feel like right now.

The broadcast jumps between flashy promotional clips and the live court feed. And, of course, the commentary keeps circling back to him.

"...Standing at 6'9", senior center Hunter Jace has been the cornerstone of Westbridge's Cinderella run this season..."

"Yeah, Chuck - averaging 21.4 points, 7.8 rebounds, and 5.2 assists per game - Jace is a true triple-threat."

"Shooting 51% from the field and 42% from beyond the arc, he's not just tall, he's efficient."

"Hunter Jace has the poise of a veteran and handles of a point guard. He's got NBA scouts on high alert tonight."

All praise. All spotlight.

I hug the blanket a little tighter around myself.

On screen, he rolls his shoulders once, jaw tight, eyes scanning the court. Focused. Controlled. And maybe even a bit nervous. It makes me smile.

It makes him seem human, and less like the basketball god he is.

Hunter doesn't do nervous. Not outwardly, anyway.

I texted him earlier, wished him luck even though he doesn't need it. He's worked so hard for this, I know he'll be great.

The camera cuts to center court.

Hunter steps into the circle for tip-off. Navy and gold against Montana's white and red. The arena roars through my laptop speakers.

I bite my lip as the referee steps in. The whistle blows.

Hunter leaps upward, long arms slicing through the air—a clean tip-off win. The game ignites instantly. Bodies streak across the hardwood, sneakers screeching as the ball zips from hand to hand. Montana comes out aggressive, pressing early. Westbridge responds just as quick.

Hunter sprints down-court like physics doesn't apply to him. He pivots. Posts up. Makes the quick pass. One clean turn. And swish. Jalen nails the first basket.

I gasp, then immediately laugh at myself, clapping alone in my dorm like a lunatic. I do a small cheer for our team. But the action continues and Montana scores right back.

I shove another handful of popcorn into my mouth, eyes glued to the screen as the score climbs on both ends.

The pace only gets faster. Montana's center is built like a brick wall—all elbows and brute strength—but Hunter doesn't flinch. He tosses a no-look assist to Jalen on the break, then plants himself on defense and draws a charge that sends the Westbridge bench leaping on their feet.

I can't help smiling. A few weeks ago, I wouldn't have understood half of that. Now I catch little details—the positioning, the reads, the timing.

"...Jace is everywhere tonight!" the commentator booms. "That's a floor general if I've ever seen one."

My fingers hover over my phone, tempted to text him, but I restrain myself. He won't answer... he's busy.

I tuck my knees under me and lean closer to my screen, nearly spilling my popcorn in the process. Then it happens.

Hunter anticipates a pass mid-court, snatches it clean out of the air, and takes off. Three long strides. One explosive leap. He slams it down with a one-handed dunk that rattles the rim.

I squeal. I *actually* squeal.

He lands, pumping his fist as the buzzer sounds to close out the first half.

"...OH MY—Hunter Jace with the steal and finish! That's a statement dunk!" the announcer shouts.

I don't even hesitate this time. I grab my phone.

Lookin' good, Hot Shot!

Halftime rolls in, and I shuffle to my mini fridge for a soda to pair with my popcorn. The sportscasters recap earlier upsets, broken brackets, and buzzer-beaters from around the country. I still don't get the bracket thing, but I nod along like I do.

My phone buzzes as I crawl back onto my bed.

The moment I see his name, a grin spreads wide across my lips.

Knowing you're watching gave me little extra pep in my step, Short-Stack.

My heart does that stupid fluttering again.

Go and kick some more ass.

On impulse, I snap a quick picture—me wrapped in his Westbridge sweatshirt, popcorn bowl in frame—and send it.

Three dots appear. Disappear. And, reappear.

All I get is a winky-face emoji.

I roll my eyes smiling away.

Halftime winds down. The players return to the court. The camera zooms in on Hunter sitting at the end of the bench, with a towel draped around his neck. He's breathing slow and focused. His coach leans in, says something. Hunter nods once, that familiar smirk tugging at his mouth.

The whistle blows.

Second half.

The ref tosses the ball up—but Montana snags possession. They score immediately. Then, they score again. My smile fades. The momentum shifts fast. Montana goes on a run, and as I watch Hunter… something feels off.

His movements aren't as sharp. He's a half-step slower. He's sweating more, chest rising harder than it did before.

My brows furrow. "What's wrong?" I whisper to myself.

The score tightens. Back and forth. Back and forth.

Then Hunter drives hard through traffic, splitting two defenders on the way, and twists mid-air for a layup—and gets hammered on the way down. He crashes to the floor as the whistle blows. The crowd erupts.

He pops up quickly, like he always does. But this time… I see it. The flicker.

His face tightens. His hand presses briefly against his sternum. He tries to play it off as he staggers to the free-throw line.

Coach McGraw is already storming onto the court, yelling.

"Hey!" Coach McGraw shouts. "Sub! Sub!"

Hunter waves him off at first, bent slightly at the waist, like he's trying to catch his breath. But he's pale. Too pale.

The ref tosses him the ball. He makes the first free throw. Barely.

The second one rims out.

He never misses like that.

The whistle blows for the sub, and he stumbles toward the bench, but his steps aren't steady. His jaw is tight, shoulders rigid.

I bolt upright, the popcorn spilling unnoticed onto my blanket. I clutch my phone to my chest.

"...Yeah, something's not quite right," one announcer says. "Look at him—he's bent over, clutching his chest again. Coach McGraw looks to be calling for a medic."

"And remember, Chuck," the other commentator adds, "a few weeks ago Hunter had that medical emergency on court. Details were never fully disclosed. I wonder if this related."

Medical incident? That's what they call it? He told me it was mid-game fatigue.

The camera zooms in briefly as a trainer reaches him on the bench. His head is down, and someone's talking to him. He nods, but it looks forced.

My throat tightens.

"Hopefully he'll be alright and able to return if Westbridge can pull this one off," the announcer continues.

They do—thankfully—pull it off. Once Hunter was out of the game, it was a little closer, but Westbridge managed to make it to the Round of 32.

The arena erupts. Confetti falls. Teammates celebrate.

But I barely register any of it.
All I can see is Hunter on the sideline.
And all I can think is—is he really okay?

CHAPTER 20

Holly

I COULDN'T BRING MYSELF to watch the second game in New York. I told myself it was because I had too much work to do. Because I needed to focus.

But that wasn't it. I couldn't watch him struggle again. They won. I know that much. Round of Sixteen. Another step closer to something massive. And every time I texted him to ask how he was, all I got back was: "I'm fine."

He's anything but.

And it makes me furious.

Tuesday evening, I'm sitting cross-legged on my bed, laptop open, half-writing a paper and half-staring at the blinking cursor when there's a knock at my door.

My brows knit together. I'm not expecting anyone. When I open the door, Hunter is standing there. Flashing his mega-watt smile.

"Hey, baby."

The sight of him, alive, here, in front of me, hits me with a wave of relief. Then, anger crashes right over it.

I frown, slamming the door in his face.

He catches it before it closes. "Whoa, whoa! What's wrong?"

He steps inside anyway, shutting and locking the door behind him.

"What's wrong?" I repeat, incredulous. "*What's wrong?* I don't know, Hunter. How about you tell me?"

He blinks, genuinely thrown. Damn him and that dashing face. But I can see it now that he's closer—the wariness in his gaze—bags under his eyes. He opens his mouth to speak.

But I interrupt before he gets a word out. "And don't you dare say you're fine," I snap. "I watched the first game. I saw you on that bench. I heard what the commentators said. So don't give me some half-assed bullshit excuse you always do."

His shoulders drop. The fight drains out of him as he sits heavily on the edge of my bed. "I didn't want to worry you," he mumbles.

I let out a sharp laugh that borders on hysterical. "You didn't want to worry me? Hunter, you scared the hell out of me... *again*! I thought you were having a heart attack on national television!" My voice cracks. Tears blur my vision before I can stop them.

"Whatever it is you're not telling me," I continue, softer now but no less intense, "I need to know. I'm not just here for the good parts, okay? You asked me to fight for us. Well, here I am. And you don't get to protect me by lying to me. Or by keeping secrets."

Hunter's gaze drops to the floor, jaw clenched as he takes a deep breath. He moves to my bed and sits, leaning forward with his elbows on his knees, dragging both hands over his face like he's trying to steady himself.

"It's my heart," he says, his voice barely above a whisper. I don't interrupt. I just wait.

"When I was in high school, I had an accident pretty similar to the one I had a few weeks ago. They ran tests. Found out I have HCM—hypertrophic cardiomyopathy."

The words hand heavy in the air. I freeze, unable to move.

He lifts his head, and his eyes are red, glassy in a way I've never seen before. "I've mostly been able to control it through diet and exercise. But lately," he swallows. "It's been acting up more. I guess it's the adrenaline and strain."

My chest tightens.

"My coaches know," he continues. "But I didn't tell anyone on the team. I didn't want to sit out. I didn't want to lose everything I've worked for..." His voice cracks.

I step forward until I'm standing between his knees. He pulls me into him immediately, arms wrapping around my waist, his forehead pressing against my shoulder like he's been holding this up alone for too long.

"Is there a cure?" I ask softly.

He shakes his head. "No. It's common in bigger athletes. The heart isn't able to support this big, huge body. The muscle inside thickens. There's medication. Monitoring. But..." He exhales shakily. "That's it."

This has been his dream. I know it. I've seen it in his eyes every time he talks about basketball.

I wrap my arms around him, cradling his head against me. His body trembles—not from pain, but from the weight of it all.

"Then we figure it out," I whisper, my voice thick. "We talk to the doctors. We take it seriously. You don't hide it. And you don't go through it alone."

He doesn't answer right away. He just holds me tighter. Like he's afraid that if he loosens his grip, everything might slip through his fingers.

"You don't get to give up, Hunter."

He pulls back just enough to look at me, eyes glassy and uncertain.

"But what if they tell me I can't play anymore?" His voice frays at the edges. "What if this is it?"

I take his hands in mine, squeezing them gently.

"Then you'll still be you," I say, offering him the smallest, steadiest smile I can manage. "You're more than basketball. More than a jersey and a scoreboard." My throat tightens. "You have a heart that's too big for your own good... literally." A tear slips down my cheek. "That heart is the reason I fell in love with you."

He swallows hard. His lips part like he wants to say something, but only a shaky breath escapes.

So I lean in and kiss him. Soft, slow and sure.

His fingers thread through my hair, like touching me is the only thing keeping him grounded.

"You're not alone in this," I whisper against his lips. "So, stop trying to lock me out and pretending you are."

Hunter stares at me, dark eyes wide and searching. "You said you love me," he breathes. "You said it..."

I blink, caught off guard by how tender his voice sounds. How broken. How hopeful.

"Yeah," I answer softly. "I did."

His eyes close briefly, like he's absorbing it. "Say it again."

I cup his face, brushing my thumbs over the damp trail of tears on his cheeks. "I love you, Hunter Jace. Every part of you. The stubborn, reckless, basketball-obsessed parts. The Mr. Darcy parts. Even the part that's vulnerable and scared sitting right in front of me."

My words seem to physically hit him. He exhales, and it's like something in him finally gives way. "I don't know what's going to happen," he admits, voice trembling. "But if I lose everything else... don't let me lose you."

I press my forehead to his. "As a wise man once said... you have me. All of me."

His breath shakes out in a soft, almost disbelieving laugh. His hands tighten at my waist, holding me like I'm the only solid thing in the room.

He exhales shakily, breath warm against my skin as I cradle his face in my hands. He still feels too warm—like adrenaline hasn't fully left his system.

"Lie down with me?" He asks quietly.

I nod without hesitation.

He shifts back onto my bed, pulling me with him until we're curled together. My head tucks beneath his chin, his arms wrapping around me like I'm the only thing keeping him steady. His heartbeat presses against my chest—strong. Fast. Alive.

My fingers drift lightly over his chest, pausing over the place that scares us both. He flinches just slightly, but he doesn't stop me.

"It's beating fast," I whisper.

"So is yours," he murmurs. "Every time you touch me, I feel like I can breathe again."

I press a soft kiss to his neck. Then another just beneath his jaw. His fingers slide just under the hem of my shirt—not urgent, not demanding—just needing contact. Skin to skin. Proof that we're still here.

This isn't wildfire. It's embers. Slow. Intentional.

Like we're reminding each other that despite the chaos, we choose this. We choose us.

"God, I'm so fucking lucky," he whispers against my temple as he pulls me on top of him. His hands are steady at my waist; his eyes never leave mine. For the first time tonight, he looks calm. Loved. Safe.

Hunter lies beneath me, his hands still gripping my waist, but he doesn't take control. He waits for me. That shift—him surrendering the lead—does something deep inside me.

I reach for the hem of my shirt and pull it slowly over my head, my eyes locked into his. His eyes darken, jaw clenches like he's holding back a prayer.

I can see the war within him. Desire tangled with need. But I don't rush. I'm here to remind him he's still alive. Still loved. Still mine.

I lean down and kiss him, slow and deep. My hands brace against his firm chest. He lets out a low groan against my mouth, one that reverberates all the way through me. I roll my hips just enough to tease him, feeling him throb against his basketball shorts, hard and ready.

"Let me take care of you," I whisper against his lips. My fingers trail slowly down his chest, hooking into the hem of his shirt before lifting it over his head. His muscles tense under my gaze as I trace my fingers along his chest.

"Holly..." it's barely a sound. More like a breath.

I press a soft kiss to the corner of his mouth to quiet him. Then along his jaw. Then lower. Slow. Sensual.

I'm unsure where this bravado is coming from, but it feels right. It feels earned.

My movements are slow and deliberate as I slide off his shorts and boxer briefs—revealing all of him. He's so beautiful like this. Naked. Vulnerable. Looking at me like I've rewritten gravity. Like I've undone him in the best possible way.

I slip out of my own clothes just as slowly, then climb back over him. For a moment, we just look at each other. Skin to skin.

My palms glide over his chest as I trace his muscle all the way down to his hip. His thumbs gently run along my bare thighs as we savor in each other. Feeling each other. Inhaling each other.

Once I feel ready, I move my hand down to his member and begin to stroke his thick, full length. Hunter hisses through gritted teeth, his eyes closing with every stroke. A curse escapes his lips as he moans my name. I can't help the amused grin that sprawls across my lips.

After teasing him just enough, I line the head of his cock to my center. The sensation of him against my entrance is heaven, and the second I sink down onto him, we both gasp. His hands start to move instinctively. But I catch them. I interlace our fingers and pin them above his head. He looks up at me, surprise flickering into heat. My entire body sprawls across him.

"No," I say, grinding my hips in a slow rhythm, allowing him deeper within me. "This is mine tonight."

It isn't about power. I just want to please him. He's been so gentle and careful with me, I want to return the favor and tend to him tonight. He looks up at me, chest heaving, eyes dark and wanting. A little smile crosses those sumptuous lips.

"Then take it," he says, voice wrecked. And I do.

I slowly roll my hips, feeling him deep inside, hitting that sacred wall that makes me moan.

It's a promise... a promise to him, that despite all of it, he's not alone. And that no matter what comes next, I'm here. Body and soul.

CHAPTER 21

Holly

I WAKE UP TANGLED in Hunter's arms, not even remembering when I fell asleep. Soft morning light spills through my window, stretching across his chest in golden bands. I rest my hand on his muscles, smiling to myself.

He shifts, his large hand covering mine as his eyes blink open.

"Mornin', Stacks," he smiles, voice thick with sleep.

"Hey, Hot Shot," I whisper back, stretching slightly.

The way his hands sprawl across the entirety of my back sends a shiver up my spine. Waking up next to him—skin to skin, no walls between us—feels addictive. I'll never get enough of this feeling. He presses a lazy kiss to my lips. Then another. The third kiss lingers deeper and longer.

Our naked bodies melt together as Hunter pulls me against him with all his strength. His palm slides down my rear, cupping my behind. I squeak, half-laughing.

He chuckles against my lips, darting his tongue out to lick my mouth.

"Such a cute little ass," he teases squeezing it again.

"Hunter," I groan as I try to roll away.

"Uh huh." His grip firms just enough to keep me where I am. "You're not getting away that easily."

His mouth trails down my neck, sucking on my shoulder before moving down my collarbone. A little moan leaves my lips as my head tilts back. Hunter grabs the back of my head, weaving his fingers through my hair giving it a light tug.

My body arches into him and in a blink, he shifts us, and suddenly I'm on my back, staring up at him. He hovers above me, eyes bright with mischief, his dark hair mussed up.

Then, slowly—sensually—his mouth maps a path down my body. As if his lips are on a mission to spend at least one full second on each spot. He kisses between my breasts, his thumbs tweak my nipples, drawing a gasp from me. He continues lower, kissing my belly button. Then lower.

"Hunter," I breathe, though I don't really mean stop.

He looks up at me, eyes dark and playful. When I don't say anything else, he resumes—lower still. The first touch of his tongue on my clit sends a jolt through me. A moan escapes my mouth as he wraps his hands around my thighs.

"Easy, baby. I got you." He whispers against my sex.

Goosebumps rise on my skin at the softness in his voice. I inhale slowly, trying to steady myself—but the moment his tongue moves again, any attempt at composure dissolves. The sensation makes me breathless. But he takes his time. Wide, flat, deliciously slow laps up and down my slit, like he's savoring every reaction. Then, Hunter inserts his tongue inside me and my walls clench. God, it feels incredible. A loud moan slips out of my mouth before I can stop it.

"Such a good girl," Hunter whispers, his tongue still assaulting me in the best way possible. "You taste so sweet."

My body shudders. His hands sprawl up my sides, those long fingers reaching out as his thumbs caress the underside of my breasts, making my body arch as I pull him in. As if challenged, he pulls my body further against his mouth, his tongue spearing me while his lips gently suck on me.

"Ah!" I yell this time, unable to keep my voice down. My body spasms, the walls around Hunter's tongue clench tighter, my fingers weaving through his hair. His hands slide down my sides and then I suddenly feel a finger, as he pulls out his tongue.

"Come on, baby. Come for me." Hunter nuzzles against my skin, kissing my body. His lips find mine almost instantly, while he inserts another finger inside me. I groan in his mouth from the sensation. My pants coming in fast.

"That's it, baby. Just let go, I got you."

He gently sucks on my neck and I am lost. My walls clench and the floodgates open as I orgasm, squeezing his fingers. I'm riding the wave of pleasure as Hunter steals the noises with his mouth.

My body flushes as I come down from the high of pleasure. "Oh god," I murmur, pushing damp hair from my forehead. Hunter crawls up my body and I feel his erection nestled between my thighs.

"You did so good, baby. I don't think I'll ever have enough of that." Hunter smiles against my mouth, following it with a sensual, drawn-out kiss.

I laugh weakly. "I'm not sure if I'm going to recover from that."

Hunter chuckles. It's warm and honest as he brushes away another strand of my hair. "I'm not quite done with you yet," he says, voice low but warm. "Roll over, baby."

I gulp, hesitating for half a second before I roll onto my stomach. In one swift motion, Hunter grabs my hips and lifts my butt in the air, my shoulders and head pressing against the bed. He shuffles as I feel the mattress dip and then I hear it. A condom wrapper being tore open. I take a deep breath and Hunter senses my anxiety.

"Don't worry, baby," he exhales onto my back, pressing soft kisses on my ass. "Just like before, I got you."

Then, I feel him. He rubs the head of his cock on my entrance a few times. The feeling eases me a bit. Then, he penetrates me, just a little at a time.

A primal moan escapes my mouth. I'm not used to this position. And, Hunter feels even bigger than usual.

"Deep breath," he reminds me gently. "It's okay. I'll go slow for you."

And he does.

He moves in rhythm with me, giving me time to adjust. He goes in just a little and then pulls out, leaving just enough of his body inside me. He works his hips slowly in tune with my body, rocking us together in a steady, building cadence. The pleasure is intoxicating.

His grip on my hips is firm as he begins to quicken the pace ever so slightly. I can feel his hips gyrate as he takes command of my body. The feeling is so deep and my hand instinctively travels to my lower belly, as if I can feel him pushing up there. After a few quick thrusts, he jolts all the way to the hilt.

"Shit—" A loud moan escapes me as he stays there for a moment.

"Oh, Holly... damn you feel so incredible." He exhales, his voice slightly strained as he explores all of me.

I glance back at him, catching a glimpse of damp hair falling into his eyes, his jaw tight with desire, his head leaned up toward the ceiling. I love to see him like this. In all his glory.

His lean muscles are so beautifully carved sometimes I wonder if they're even real. A sheen of sweat glistens along his firm chest.

Once he takes a breath, he resumes his pace. Slow at first, but then he quickens. Relentless. He finds a rhythm that blurs everything—the room, the light, the outside world. His bruising grip on my hips pulls me into his thrusts making his cock to hit a wall within me. And I am nothing but a puddle. Molten liquid in his hands. My body just accepting and stretching and loving every minute of it.

Hunter lightly shakes my hips as he continues thrusting me. I feel it building again. The walls clenching, the dam breaking. And I'm undone. Again. He follows close behind me, a low, broken sound spilling from him as he presses forward and then stills.

The room settles into the sound of our breathing—uneven at first, then gradually slowing. Coming down from the high of our orgasms. Slowly, Hunter pulls out and then removes the condom. He tosses it into the trash can by my bed and slides beside me, pulling me into his arms. He kisses me softly. I rest my hand against his chest—and immediately feel it. Beating fast, almost erratically.

"Are you okay?" I ask, my voice lower now.

Hunter smiles, brushing his thumb along my jaw. "Better than okay, baby."

"Your heart—"

"Is fine," he finishes my sentence lifting my hand to press a kiss against my knuckles.

I search his face, "Are you sure?"

Hunter laughs, running a hand through his hair. "Holly, if I die making love to you, than it'd be completely worth it."

I smack his chest lightly. "That is not funny!"

He hums, wrapping his arms tighter around me. "It's hilarious. But, also true, baby. That'd be a great way to go."

"Please stop saying that." My eyes begin to burn.

Hunter notices immediately.

"No, don't cry, Holly," he whispers, wiping the tear before it can fall. "I'm alright. I'm here. I'm not going anywhere. Not yet, okay?" He presses a gentle kiss to the side of my lip. I nod, because if I try to speak, I might unravel.

"How about we get cleaned up and I take you to the Nest for breakfast?" Hunter asks, his forehead pressed to mine.

I sniffle, rubbing my nose. A small laugh escapes me despite everything. "Yeah, that sounds good."

"Great," he says with a grin. "Cause I'm starving." I roll my eyes grinning with him. He gives me another kiss as he rolls out of bed and starts getting dressed.

CHAPTER 22

Holly

I WRAP MY HANDS around my caramel latte, letting the warmth seep into my fingers as I watch Hunter across the table. The Nest feels different this morning. Softer. Warm golden light spills from amber Edison bulbs, indie music humming beneath the quiet chatter of early risers.

Hunter looks wildly out of place in the tiny wooden chair. His knees wedge awkwardly beneath the table. I bite back a laugh as he shifts, trying to fold himself smaller.

"So," he says casually. "I'd really love for you to come to Nashville for the Sweet Sixteen."

I pause mid-sip. "Hunter—"

"I know, I know," he cuts in, grinning. "You have classes and work and all these things. But, is there any way you could swing it? It's way closer than New York." He gives me that ridiculous, cheesy smile like proximity alone should seal the deal.

I lower my mug, and rest my chin in my hands. "It is. But unless you've forgotten, I don't have a car. How exactly am I supposed to get there, Hot Shot?"

Hunter opens his mouth, then shuts it as our food arrives.

"Thank you," I murmur as the lady sets down my Nutella and peanut butter crepe. Hunter's quiche lands between his massive hands, steam curling up between us.

He takes a bite, chewing thoughtfully.

Then—like it's obvious—he says, "You could take the charter."

I blink. "The what?"

"The school's running a couple charter buses for students who want to go to the game." He shrugs. "I could probably pull a few strings. Snag you a seat. And a ticket to the game."

My fork still hovers in the air as I stare at him. "You want me to go on a bus full of total strangers for four hours and then walk into a huge crowded stadium alone?" I ask, incredulous. "You know that's an anxiety attack waiting to happen."

He lifts one broad shoulder. "It's an option." Then that slow grin spreads across his face. "I promise I'd make it worth your while."

My brow arches. "Oh? How so?"

He makes a dramatic thinking face, tapping his chin. "That's for me to know... and you to potentially find out."

I roll my eyes, groaning softly. "You're ridiculous."

"But you like it," he counters easily.

"I'll think about it," I sigh cutting into my crepe. "Won't your parents be there? Don't you want to spend time with them?"

His smile brightens. "They will. And I will, beforehand. But I also want you there." His voice is laced with sincerity.

"What time is the game?" I ask, trying to sound casual. "I'm scheduled to work Saturday."

His smile fades. "Can you switch with someone?" There's almost something desperate in his tone now.

I hum exaggeratedly, imitating him from earlier. "That's for me to know and you to find out."

He chuckles, low and warm. "Careful."

"Careful?" I repeat.

He leans across the table, invading my space with effortless confidence. His mouth hovers near my ear, voice dropping to a murmur. "If we weren't in public... I'd find a very convincing way to get that answer out of you."

Heat floods my cheeks, but I refuse to him the satisfaction. "You wouldn't hurt a fly," I challenge.

His hand slides just above my bare knee under the table. Goosebumps race up my thigh. When I meet his eyes, they're darker now—determined.

"Do I need to carry you out of here caveman style and prove you wrong?" he asks, voice deep and teasing all at once. My stomach flutters traitorously.

I take another sip of my latte, shaking my head.

"You sure?" he teases. Considering I'm still sore from last night and this morning? Yeah, I'm pretty sure. But maybe I don't mind testing him a little.

"I don't know," I say lightly. "All I know is that I'm enjoying my latte with my boyfriend, and I'd like to enjoy it a little longer before he goes all caveman on me." His expression changes. There's a hungry, salacious look in his eyes.

"Say it again," he murmurs. I almost miss it. But when our eyes lock, I see the hunger in them.

I smirk. Let him wait, take another slow sip of my latte, deliberately licking the foam from my top lip. His eyes dart to my tongue.

"My boyfriend," I whisper.

He scarfs down the rest of his quiche in like two bites and stands. The sudden movement startles me, but when he offers his hand, I take it. He almost drags me out of the café, his grip hurried yet warm.

We cross Bridge Street and cut toward campus. His long strides eat up the pavement, and I have to half-jog to keep up.

"Hunter!" I call out, breathless. "What's wrong?"

He doesn't answer. He crosses the Quad and heads straight for my dorm.

When we reach the doors, he spins on his heel, eyes wild in a way that makes heat curl low in my stomach.

"Open the door, Holly." It's a command.

I fumble for my ID and scan us in. He keeps a hand on the small of my back as we move through the vintage lobby and up the stairs. My room is on the fifth floor, the top.

By the time we reach my door, I'm winded. "Jesus, Hunter... give me a second. I'm not as in shape as you."

He literally grabs the key chain out of my hand and unlocks the door. Once inside, he shuts it firmly behind us. We're locked.

He spins and pins me to the door, caging me in. My breath stutters. I feel small under his shadow. Maybe because I am. My five-foot five stature has nothing on him.

Tenderly, he brushes a strand of hair from my face and tucks it behind my ear before sliding the same hand to the back of my neck. His thumb strokes along my jawline. My lips part automatically.

The silence between us thickens. Not tense. But charged.

He watches me like he's deciding something.

Every nerve in my body sparks under the slow drag of his thumb.

"What's wrong Hunter?" I whisper. "What do you need?"

"You," he replies softly. "Just you, baby."

The words ghost over my lips before his mouth replaces them. It's slow at first. Tender and warm and everything a girl could ever want.

I rise onto my toes to deepen the kiss, and he responds instantly by wrapping his arms around me as he lifts me with effortless strength.

I yelp in surprise, but then wrap my legs around his waist. I can feel his erection as he presses his muscular body against mine.

"I can't get enough of you," he breathes, almost pained. "Do you have any idea what you do to me?"

He grinds his hips once, just enough to make his meaning clear. My skirt rides higher as his hands grasp the skin beneath my thighs.

I grab his face, pressing our foreheads, "I do."

"Fuck." His voice drops, rougher now. "Say that again."

"I do." I say hesitantly, unsure why that sets him off.

His mouth claims mine again, deeper this time, teeth grazing, tongue demanding. He holds me with one hand and I feel him shifting. It isn't until I feel his fingers sliding my panties aside do I realize what's going on.

He thrusts into me in one swift motion. I moan, my head falling back as he hits my inner wall. When I think I can't take any more of him, he thrusts up further.

"Shit," I gasp, fingers digging into his shoulders.

"You take me so well," he grunts, his thrusts going deeper than I thought was possible. The stretching, the burning, the pleasure, it all melts into something molten and consuming. When my eyes sting unexpectedly, he notices. His thumb brushes beneath my eye. "You okay, baby?" he murmurs, his voice soothing. "You're doing so good. Do you need me to stop?"

"No!" The word tears out of me. "Don't you dare."

A dark sound leaves his chest—half laugh, half growl.

He picks up his pace, and I hang onto his neck; my nails dig into his muscular back. The sound of our skin meeting is crude and wet and just when I feel the tidal wave building and building, Hunter leans back, ever so slightly. The minute the angle changes, he hits my g-spot and I shatter.

CHAPTER 23

Holly

I'M WEDGED INTO A stale charter bus that smells faintly of sweat and something worse, surrounded by rowdy Westbridge students chanting like their lives depend on it.

They've been at it for two hours. How are they not tired? How do they still have voices?

I try to focus on the book Hunter bought me at the Nook—cute, bright, annoyingly cheerful—but the noise makes it impossible. After another thirty minutes of relentless singing, I give up. I slide the book back into my satchel and curl my legs to my chest, staring out the window instead.

The game is in a few hours. I wonder what he's doing. Before I can stop myself, I grab my phone.

How long is this bus ride again?

You mean to tell me you're not having the time of your life? Beer funnels? Fight songs?

Oh, there's singing. It hasn't stopped. For over *two* hours!

A few minutes pass.

I hope you're leading it.

I groan.

My eyes just rolled so far in the back of my head that they might be stuck.

Oh, Short-Stack. Sounds like you deserve a big hug when I see you.

That, and then some…

When there's no flirty response from him, I text again.

What are you doing?

Naughty Short-Stack. On the bus?

I pause, unsure the innuendo, until it hits me that my previous text sounded like a late-night booty call.

Gross, Hunter. Absolutely not. I'm just curious.

Well…just pregame stuff. Not sure if you'd want details.

I stare at the screen. Did he just—

The thought slips in before I can stop it. Hunter alone somewhere, focused, stroking himself...

Just by thinking of it, heat curls low in my stomach, briefly drowning out the chanting around me.

I snap out of it. I'm sure it'd be the most beautiful thing I'd ever see. But I'm on a damn bus. With screaming strangers. I force myself to look out the window instead.

Did I lose you there, baby?

Sorry...Bad connection out here.

Lie. I can feel the blush creeping up my neck. I'm not admitting what I was actually thinking about.

You'll let me know when you get here?

I will.

I can't wait, baby.

Finally, we roll into Nashville after the longest four hour and thirteen minute of my life. The second bus doors open, students pour out, cheering like we've already won.

I step down more cautiously. Nashville is loud. Neon signs blaze against the afternoon sky. Music spills from somewhere nearby. The air smells like smoke and barbecue and traffic.

And then I see it. Bridgestone Arena stands in front of me, all glass and steel at an impossible scale. Bigger than anything I've stood in front of. It almost looks futuristic—like something dropped from space into the middle of downtown.

Police line the streets. Cars inch past. Thousands of people move in waves of navy and gold. I'm one of them. Hunter's jersey hangs slightly oversized on me, lucky number thirteen stretched across my back.

I feel... exposed. Proud even. And completely out of place.

For a second, I just spin in a slow circle, taking it all in. The noise. The motion. The magnitude of it all.

What am I doing here?

I scan for the students from my bus, and spot a cluster of familiar jerseys heading toward one of the entrances. I fall in behind them, pretending I know exactly where I'm going.

Inside, everything is even louder.

I pull the ticket from my bag—the one that Hunter pressed into my hand before he left. It states "WESTBRIDGE STUDENT SECTION" on the top, followed by a section, row, and seat number.

Thankfully, the signage is clear, and I let it guide me through the maze of corridors and stairwells.

People brush past me on all sides—laughing, shouting, already a little drunk.

The smell of beer and popcorn overwhelms me. For a second, I consider skipping the food line. But I don't. If I'm doing this, I'm doing it properly.

I grab a diet coke and popcorn and cling to them like armor as I finally climb toward my seat.

I'm surrounded by Westbridge students in a sea of navy and gold. Jerseys. Face paint. Full-blown costumes. Poster boards held high like battle flags.

I can't help smiling. Being in the thick of it is strangely exhilarating. A little overwhelming, yes. But manageable.

A few weeks ago, I would've melted down in a crowd like this.

I quickly pull out my phone and text him.

Made it. See you on the court, Hot Shot.

No response. I didn't expect one. But, at least he knows I'm here and safe.

Music pounds through the arena, bass vibrating up through the soles of my shoes and into my ribs. Massive screens flash highlight reels and dramatic slow-motion shots. The sound, the light, the sheer scale of it all makes my pulse quicken.

This place dwarfs our school arena. It feels important.

A promo video begins and Hunter's face fills the screen. The crowd around me bursts into screams and cheers. I bite my lip as I watch it. He looks so damn calm and collected. So cool, almost untouchable.

It's surreal knowing that the man who looks like that on a forty-foot screen is the same one who presses his forehead to mine and asks if I'm okay. He's my boyfriend.

When the lights dim, the announcer's voice booms through the stadium, introducing the number two seed holder Baylor first. Their crowd erupts. Fireworks spark at the tunnel entrance as their players storm onto the court, their bear mascot waving a massive green flag behind them. They're loud. Probably the majority here.

The lights cut again.

"Let's go, Westbridge!" someone screams behind me, and I jump as drums thunder from our small band. As our team is introduced, pyrotechnics flare up.

Hunter jogs onto the court with the rest of the team, shoulders loose, expression set.

When his name echoes through the arena, the roar is deafening. The sound reverberates in my chest. And before I realize it, I'm on my feet too—shouting, cheering, claiming him with the rest of them.

Hunter unzips his warm-up jacket, revealing the familiar number thirteen stretched across his chest. The same one resting over my heart.

Heat flares in my chest as I absently brush my fingers over the fabric of my jersey. He looks different out there. Focused. Locked in.

The playful ease I know is gone, replaced by that stone-cold, jaw-clenched intensity I've only ever seen in his highlights.

He doesn't look at me, obviously. There is no way he could pick me out in the massive crowd. Still, my eyes stay glued to him the entire time.

The student section grows louder, bodies pressing closer as chants start up again. The energy is bigger here than it ever was in the VIP section. No buffer. No quiet distance. Just noise, and heat, and commotion. My chest tightens.

"Okay," I murmur to myself. "Breathe. You're here for him. You can do this."

On the court, the teams finish their warm-ups and gather at the center. Baylor wins the tip. Our section erupts in boos, but I stay quiet, focusing on slow steady breaths.

Then, Hunter glances toward the crowd. For a split second, I think it's coincidence. There are too many people. Too much distance. But his gaze lingers. And I feel it. Like the air shifted.

His expression changes—barely. A flicker at the corner of his mouth. The faintest hint of a smirk. Then, the little wink.

It was subtle and quick, yet deliberate. It was for me.

My heart kicks harder against my ribs—not from anxiety this time, but something steadier. I feel my fists easing, the tension dissipating just a little. Because even in a stadium packed with thousands, he still knows exactly where I am.

CHAPTER 24

Hunter

I DON'T KNOW HOW I found her in a stadium packed with thousands. But I did.

It was like a spotlight shining down upon her amidst the tournament chaos. My eyes wandered into the crowd, and there she was. My Holly girl. Standing in the middle of all that madness, looking overwhelmed and so out of place. And still the most incredible thing in the building.

She came. She got on that bus. Sat through God knows how many hours of chanting and cheap beer fumes. Stepped *way* out of her comfort zone. For me.

My chest tightens. Not in a bad way. Just... full.

I need to do something special for her. Something big. Something she won't expect. Later.

Right now, Baylor—our toughest opponent yet—is staring us down across the court. They're not here for a cute underdog story. We may be the number three seed, but they're number two.

They fought hard, they're fast and they have a solid defense.

We're good too. But tonight, good won't be enough. I need to play clean. Smart. And it can't just be me. If we win this, it's because every guy in navy shows up.

Coach McGraw, Raymond—the other team captain—and I step to the center court for the toss. Raymond's also a senior and one of our key defensive guys. The main ref joins us. After his usual coin toss spiel, he flips it.

"Tails," I call.

It lands. Heads. Damnit. Baylor picks their hoop, and we reset for tip-off.

"Alright, gentlemen, let's have a clean game. Jump straight up. No early contact. I'll toss it high, go on the way down. Play hard, play fair. Ready?"

I nod, heart hammering. Light on my feet, knees bent, I wait.

The ref launches the ball. Everything narrows. I explode upward and tip it cleanly to our side. Victory number one.

Jalen pushes the pace immediately, weaving past his defender as I sprint down-court and plant myself in the paint. Benny, our 6'3" shooting guard, gets the pass and pulls up. The shot rattles.

I'm already there.

One quick extension of my arm—soft touch off the glass. And in. First points.

The roar hits a second later, rolling through the arena like thunder. It's always thrilling to get those first points, but there's no time to enjoy it. I pivot and run.

Baylor moves the ball fast. Toss – dribble – toss – dribble, dribble – toss. My guys contest everything, but they stay patient.

Their small forward rises for a jumper. I get a hand on it—just enough to alter the arc. Their center rebounds and slams it home.

Tie game. Back and forth.

I dash to our end. Jalen speeds across, and dishes to Drake—our small forward—who nails a three from the wing.

We reset again. No whistles, no easy mistakes. Just bodies colliding and sneakers squealing against hardwood.

The ball roams between different hands, different teams. Thirty seconds of chaos with no score.

The Baylor guard crosses half court, offense setting up quick. I sink lower in the paint, eyes tracking the ball. My assignment is their bulky forward with surprisingly quick feet. He hovers near the elbow, eyeing the lane.

"Watch the screen!" I yell as their wing cuts hard.

Jalen fights over it. The point guard whips the ball wide. Sharp pass. Quick jab step. Their shooting guard rises for a deep two. Clean release.

I plant early, ready for the rebound. The shot clangs off the back iron—high and hard. I misjudge it. So does Benny. The ball ricochets into open space.

"Shit."

A Baylor forward crashes in untouched.

"Box out!" I shout, too late. One pump fake; a power step. The Baylor forward banks it in from under the rim. Two more points for them.

I smack the padding under the basket as the ref signals the bucket.

Baylor takes the lead.

"Come on." I growl, already turning up-court. "Lock in, guys!"

Their crowd surges, chanting, but I block it out.

I won't let the sting of the last possession settle. Not now. Not in the Sweet Sixteen.

I sprint back, dropping into the low post as Jalen crosses half court. Motion offense kicks in—Benny curling off Drake's screen, defenders shifting.

"Seal him, Hunt!" Benny calls.

I pivot hard, catching their big off balance. He presses into my back. I sink lower, widen my stance, hand up.

"Here!"

Jalen sees it. One hard bounce. Crisp entry pass.

The ball lands in my hands like it belongs there.

I fake baseline, spin middle, and elevate.

Contact.

No whistle.

Doesn't matter.

I power through it, lay it in with my left hand.

Two points.

The Westbridge student section detonates behind the basket, stomping and hooting. As I backpedal, I catch a flash of navy and gold. Holly. On her feet.

I don't let myself linger. I lock onto their center instead. "Let's dance, pretty boy."

They push the tempo off the inbound, trying to answer quick. Their point guard darts up the sideline, but Jalen cuts him off clean. Then a lazy cross-court pass. Drake reads it instantly.

He jumps the lane, tipping the pass before securing it clean. One dribble, two. He fires it ahead as I cut through the paint. I catch on the move, pivot under the rim.

Up to finish—*WHAM*!

The Baylor forward collides into me midair. I slam hard into the padded stanchion. The whistle shrieks as everything slows around me.

"FOUL!" The ref calls out, his arm slicing through the air.

I land awkwardly, one hand slapping the hardwood to steady myself. My chest is heaving. Too fast. And not just fast. It's arrhythmic—weird.

I pull in a deep breath. It doesn't settle. Jalen's hand appears in front of me. "You good?"

I nod before I fully know if it's true and let him haul me up. The crowd roars, but the sound feels distant. Muffled behind the thud in my ears.

I roll my shoulders once. Focus. The guys try to amp me up as I walk to the line.

Two shots. And we need both.

I plant my feet, bounce the ball twice, and exhale slowly.

"Punk ass don't belong here."

I glance sideways. Their center stands just outside the lane, leaning in like we're teammates instead of rivals. His demeanor cool. His words—sharp, biting.

"Cinderella's midnight is coming," he adds quietly. "Then it's back to that pumpkin school of yours."

My nostrils flare, but I don't flinch. I won't get pulled into that bullshit.

I dribble once more and fix my eyes the hoop.

The words don't hurt. But they light something.

I sink the first free throw. Clean.

Our section erupts. Drums pound behind me, the rhythm nearly matching the uneven beat in my chest. The center then huffs beside me, a sort of chuckle.

"One shot don't make you a baller," he mutters.

My jaw tightens. I'm doing everything I can not to punch the guy in the face. I know he's trying to rattle me, to throw me off my game. I won't let him.

I meet his eye this time. "You'll remember me on the bus ride home."

I swish the second free throw.

Westbridge takes the lead.

CHAPTER 25

Holly

When Hunter sinks the second free throw, the crowd erupts again. But he doesn't look happy about it. He looks pissed. You'd think he'd be celebrating—he scored, Westbridge is back on top—but something in his expression feels off.

Coach McGraw calls a timeout. The guys gather around as he scribbles across his whiteboard. I notice he motions for Hunter to sit.

When he slammed into that pole, I saw the air leave his lungs. I saw how long it took him to recover. It scared me. It still does. I know how much this game means to him, but I don't want him pushing past his limits. He has a team. They can carry some of the weight.

I'm grateful coach makes him sit for a few minutes—to breathe and reset.

I wish I could go down there. Hug him. Kiss him. Do anything to ease the tension pulling tight across his shoulders.

Instead, I'm stuck in the stands, my focus no longer on the game.

As the clock winds down, I see him itching to get back in. I glance at the scoreboard.

WESTBRIDGE: 19 BAYLOR: 23

We've fallen behind. There's work to do, and I know he wants to be the one to do it. Three minutes left in the first half. After a few more seconds, Coach McGraw nods at him.

Hunter's back in.

He looks better now and I can tell he's amped up. The crowd goes wild at his reentry.

A loud "HUNTER" chant fills the arena. He lifts his arms, urging them louder, feeding off the energy. I can't help but join in. And then he takes over.

Dunk after dunk. Power and precision. I stare at the force of him, at the beast he becomes on the court. Baylor reciprocates each time, but we start inching closer to a tie.

Jalen races down the court as the clock ticks under ten seconds. He dishes it out. A three goes up—

Misses.

The buzzer blares, signaling halftime. Cheers mix with boos as fans spill into the aisles in search of snacks and bathrooms.

I pull out my phone, tempted to text him. I stop myself though. He doesn't need distractions. Not when they're still down by two points.

Instead, I head toward the bathroom and then the concession stand. The arena hums with adrenaline. Fans from both teams argue plays and stats.

Hunter's name floats through the noise as I pass. Every time I hear it, I smile.

Hunter Jace. *My* Hunter Jace.

I make my way to the bathroom—of course there's a line. Then to a snack stall—another long one. By the time I reach the front, I'm starving. My stomach growls at the sight of popcorn and pretzels. I buy both. And a diet coke. Balancing everything, I weave back toward my seat.

I miss tip-off, but catch the action as I squeeze through the student section. The people beside me are on their feet, yelling as our team dominates the court. My eyes search for Hunter immediately.

I find him stalking into the "paint"—his paint—chest rising, jersey clinging to him like armor. I'm completely enamored.

His energy is different now. He looks harder, sharper, so focused that I couldn't distract him even if I tried. Gone is the teasing guy who handed me his jersey and made me blush for days.

This was the beast version of Hunter. The "on-fire" Hunter. All purpose. All steel.

Baylor fans boo as he fights for position beneath the hoop. There's a whistle. Offensive foul.

He doesn't react. No crack in his expression. No smile. He just turns, jaw flexing and resets for the next play. I press a hand to my chest, trying to catch my breath. God, he's beautiful even when he's furious.

The game doesn't slow down. If anything, it gets more brutal. Shouts ricochet across the court. Sneakers screech. Bodies collide.

Baylor is relentless. Westbridge has to be perfect to stay in it.

Their guard drives the lane, slicing past Jalen. The crowd rises with the tension.

But Hunter steps in at the last second—like a storm breaking through the paint.

One giant leap. Arms extended. Fingers wide.

Block!

The ball smashes off the backboard like a cannon blast. Gasps and screams of excitement fill the arena.

I jump to my feet as Hunter snatches the rebound midair and pivots. He fires the ball down-court to Benny, already sprinting. A bullet pass that splits Baylor in two.

Seconds later, Westbridge scores on a fast break. But I don't cheer. Not yet.

Hunter is still planted under the basket. His chest rises like he can't pull in air fast enough. Jaw clenched. Lips parted. Eyes dark. He isn't celebrating. He's seething. Controlled. Coiled. Like one wrong move would set him off.

He's so goddamn hot!

I swallow hard as I study this Hunter. My pulse races and I feel desire growing inside me. I want to know this side of him. This determined, dominant man, ready to wreak havoc. It's alluring in a way I can't explain. I'm not sure why it's turning me on, but I can feel my face flushing.

As Baylor moves to inbound, the pass goes sloppy. Drake intercepts it clean, ripping it from their power forward and feeding it straight to Hunter. He doesn't hesitate.

He slams it home.

He celebrates with a fist pump and a raw scream, sweat flying from his hairline. Baylor barely reacts. They reset and keep going.

The game stays neck and neck—never more than a point or two apart. Everyone in the arena is on their feet, the noise crashing from both sides.

The atmosphere is electric.

Minutes tick away as the teams battle back and forth. A whistle here. A foul there. Free throws made. Free throws missed.

I'm sitting now, foot tapping vigorously. My nerves spike with every shot.

I was never a basketball girl. Sports never called to me.

But being here for Hunter has changed something. In the weeks we've known each other, I've learned this is more than just sweaty guys sprinting across polished wood. It's discipline. Pressure. Heat.

In a way, I'm not just here for him. I'm here for me. Somewhere along the way, I've stepped out of the tiny little shell I built around myself.

Perhaps, I'm a basketball girl now. Somehow, I've happily become one.

The thrill of the game thrums through me. Maybe it's because I admire him so much. Watching him do what he loves is so fulfilling.

When he's up, I soar.

When he's frustrated, I burn.

When he's hurting, I ache.

I shake my head at myself, almost laughing.

How did this happen? How did I fall so fast for a star basketball player?

And how did he find, and choose me?

I refocus as number thirteen sprints down the court. Hunter shadows his man, towering over their center. His arms stretch wide, ready to deflect anything near the paint.

The pass goes inside.

Hunter slaps it down, corrals the ball, and pushes it out to Jalen. Jalen drives, swings it to Benny. Benny to Drake. Drake back to Jalen—

Three.

It hits!

The arena explodes again. I jump up, cheering—and send the rest of my popcorn flying into the air. No one cares. They're all too excited to care.

The score is tied.

Five minutes left.

My heart pounds so hard against my chest, that it feels like it's climbing into my throat. I can only image what the players feel.

I find myself on my feet again, rocking back and forth, chewing at my thumbnail.

"Come on, Hunter," I whisper.

Baylor answers immediately with a three-pointer. I curse under my breath, the points feeling like a punch to the gut. Their fans erupt in smug cheers, but I block them out. The game is far from over.

Westbridge pushes the pace. The Elite Eight is within their grasp.

Benny's shot leaves his hands clean and perfect. I hold my breath—

Clang!

It ricochets off the rim.

Another curse slips out my mouth. But Hunter is there. He wouldn't give up.

He battles for the rebound like a man possessed. The tip-out? The scramble? It's all elbows and hands and pure instinct.

And somehow, he has the ball.

Relief floods me. He goes back up and scores. I jump to my feet, only to hear the shriek of a whistle. Contact.

Hunter lands flat on his back beneath the basket. My stomach drops.

His chest heaves and his face is unreadable.

Benny hauls him up with a grin, but Hunter doesn't smile back. He glances at the scoreboard, then his bench, and then Baylor's. For the briefest second, his gaze sweeps the crowd. I want him to see me. I don't know if he does.

But God, I see him.

And I'll never forget this version of him. Not ever.

That look—pure focus. Raw strength. Relentless determination.

Everything around me fades, though I know it's just in my head. The only thing I hear is the steady, heavy rhythm of my own heartbeat.

Hunter walks to the free-throw line like he owns it. Shoulders squared, the ball resting in his hands like it weighs nothing. Like he's done this a thousand times.

He probably has. But not like this. Not with the score this tight. Not with the stakes this high. Not with a completely sold-out arena in Nashville screaming.

He bounces the ball once, twice. I don't move. I barely breathe.

A jeer cuts through the noise to my left.

"Bet he bricks it!"

Laughter follows. I don't turn to glare, even though I want to.

Hunter exhales, slow and steady. Then he arches up and releases.

The ball arcs cleanly, spinning in perfect silence through the air.

Everything slows as I hold my breath. My heart thuds so loudly, I'm sure the people around me can hear it.

Swish.

It goes in.

Westbridge fans erupt, but I'm frozen. Still not breathing.

The score flashes.

76-76.

Hunter steps up for his second free throw.

Two dribbles, a deep breath and release.

The ball circles the rim and slips out.

He misses.

I exhale in disappointment.

Not at him. Never at him.

I just wish something—anything—had gone wrong so he could have that shot back. But the game barrels on. Baylor scores. Then again. The clock keeps bleeding down as their lead stretches.

WESTBRIDGE: 76 BAYLOR: 79.

"Come on," I mutter, a nervous wreck.

We block their next shot and answer with a two. Down by one.

"Come on, come on," I repeat under my breath, rocking forward as the tension spikes.

Baylor scores, then Westbridge answers. Thirty seconds left.

I'm not even playing, and I'm sweating.

Drake fouls their center.

Free throws for Baylor.

Then Baylor's forward fouls Benny.

More free throws.

Players start fouling out. Rotations shift. Whistles slice through every possession. I don't understand all of it, but I desperately pray that we pull this off.

After what feels like endless stoppages, the scoreboard reads:

WESTBRIDGE: 82 BAYLOR: 83

With just seconds left on the clock now, Baylor goes up for a three. Miss.

Hunter snags the rebound and immediately outlets to Jalen before sprinting up-court. They swing the ball around—Jalen to Benny, Benny to Drake, Drake to Chris, back to Jalen.

What are they doing?

Just throw the ball!

The game clock bleeds. The shot clock is nearly gone.

"Shoot!" I whisper harshly, gripping the front of my jersey.

At the last possible second, Benny launches it from deep.

The buzzer blares.

The entire arena watches the ball hang in the air.

It hits the rim, taking a slow turnabout on it before going in.

Three points.

WESTBRIDGE WINS

CHAPTER 26

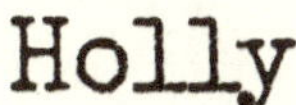

WE JUMP UP SCREAMING. I'm hugging total strangers. The players are shouting, celebrating. Navy and gold confetti rains down from cannons high above us.

The student section surges forward.

Before I can think, I'm swept into the wave, jostled as everyone floods the court. I don't even feel my feet moving, it's as if I'm floating.

And then I'm there. On the court.

Hundreds of Westbridge students spill across the hardwood, hugging players, coaches, anyone within reach. In the distance, I spot Hunter climbing the ladder, cutting down the net. Teammates crowd around him as he does.

When he drops back down, he's grinning, talking, being pulled in every direction. I suddenly feel small in the chaos.

What am I supposed to do? Go to him? Try to fight my way back to my seat—if that's even possible? Head toward the bench?

Instead, I freeze.

My heart pounds. My breathing turns shallow. The crowd presses in from every direction.

If I move, I might get trampled. But if I stay, I'll disappear. Should I head back toward the charter bus?

Strong, sweaty arms wrap around me from behind. I gasp as I'm lifted clean off the ground. Hunter spins me around, and presses his lips on mine, in a long, drawn-out, victory kiss.

I melt into him, my arms locking around his damp neck. He smells like sweat and adrenaline but beneath it there's still that faint scent of his cologne.

I come to my senses when he finally pulls back, still holding me up high against his chest, staring at me like I just hit the winning shot.

"You guys did it!" I laugh. "You made the Elite Eight."

"Fuck, Holly... we fucking did!" Hunter says, still half in shock. He kisses me again as reporters and cameras swarm around us. My cheeks burn. He sets me down, though his hands linger at my waist like he's reluctant to let go.

Someone tosses him a t-shirt with "Westbridge State Elite 8 2025" painted on it, and a matching hat.

All at once, reporters crowd him. He pulls me flush against his side as mics and cameras are shoved in his face.

"How does it feel to make Westbridge history as the first team to reach the Elite 8?" one reporter asks.

"Incredible," Hunter replies, still breathless. "I'm so thankful for my coaches and my team. These guys are unreal, and Baylor played a hell of a game. Honestly, I'm still soaking it in. Still in shock." He grins. "But we made it!"

He shouts the last bit gazing at his team. His teammates whoop behind him.

"What was going through your mind in those final moments?" another reporter calls out.

He exhales, flashing an easy smile. "I don't know. I just knew I had to play as hard as I could. Missing that free throw didn't feel great. I felt like I let my team down for a second. But you know, you can't dwell on it. You reset. You keep going. That's something I'll clean up before the next round."

After a few more questions, he finally slips away, lacing his fingers through mine and pulling me with him.

"Where are we going?" I ask once the crowd thins. "I should probably catch the charter bus back. Otherwise I won't have a ride."

He doesn't answer. Just keeps guiding me across the court and into the tunnel the team came through. The noise dulls the second we step inside.

Before I can say anything else, he backs me against the wall, and kisses me again. Deep and passionate. His hands frame my face, thumbs pressing into my cheeks as he leans down. He tastes like adrenaline and victory.

"I want you with me," he growls.

His whole body is vibrating, still riding the high.

I shake my head gently. "Maybe that's not a good idea," I quietly say. "You need to come down from this. And I need to get home."

A four plus hour bus ride sounds brutal right now, but so does being caught up in whatever wildfire is burning through him. He grabs the back of my head, fingers weaving through my hair. Goosebumps ripple down my arms as he tightens his hold slightly.

"I want you with me," he repeats, lower this time. "I don't care about anything else."

I shrug, unsure. "Hunter, where would I go? How would I get back to campus?"

He leans in closer, lips brushing my ear. "Stay at the hotel with me tonight. We drive back in the morning."

"I highly doubt your coaches are going to let me hop on the team's bougie charter bus," I say. "I don't want to miss my ride if I'm not guaranteed a way home."

His whole-body lifts in a frustrated shrug. He rests his forehead against mine.

"I don't want to get you in trouble," I add. "And aren't you sharing a room with one of the guys? I doubt your teammate wants me crashing in there. That'd be awkward. For everyone." I try to lighten it with a small laugh, but Hunter isn't amused.

"Let me shower and change," he says. "We still have the team press conference. Just sit outside the locker room. I'll sort something out, alright?"

There's almost something desperate in his eyes now. Intense. Unyielding.

I sigh. "Okay."

He grabs my hand again and leads me deeper into the tunnel, into the underbelly of the arena. The shift is jarring. Gone is the roar and color. Down here, it's nothing but gray concrete and exposed ceiling beams. Industrial lighting. The air smells like dust and sweat, instead of beer and popcorn.

When we reach a door labeled "Visiting Team", he guides me to a narrow bench just down the hall.

"Wait here. I'll be back soon, okay?" he says, giving my hand a kiss before letting go and heading toward the locker room.

I simply nod my head and wait as he disappears inside.

CHAPTER 27

Hunter

I STRIDE INTO THE locker room, giving Holly one last longing glance before the door swings shut. The room erupts with cheers the second I step inside.

Guys are shouting, blasting music, chest-bumping like we just won the whole damn tournament. I jump in with them, yelling, laughing, adrenaline still buzzing through my veins. We fucking did it. By some basketball miracle, we pulled it off. Caused the upset. It's the greatest moment of my life.

Coach McGraw storms in a minute later, shouting loud enough to cut through the chaos before motioning for us to settle down. "Guys, that was incredible!" he says, grinning. "I'm proud of each one of you. That was a hard-fought battle. You gave it all out there, and it showed. Congratulations!"

We cheer again.

"Alright now, listen up," he says, raising his voice. "We're staying tonight and heading home tomorrow. Celebrate. Do what you need to do. But you better be on that bus at seven a.m. sharp. Understood?"

"Yes, sir," we answer in unison.

"Good. Shower up. Conference in fifteen."

The room breaks apart again, guys grabbing towels and shower kits.

Instead of joining them, I head straight for coach. "Coach," I call out.

He turns, smiling. "Hey, big guy. Hell of a game." He pats my back. He's at least eight inches shorter than me.

"Thanks," I hesitate. "I was wondering if you'd consider letting one more person ride the bus tomorrow."

His brow lifts. "Who?"

I bite back a grin. "My girl's here tonight. I want to stay with her. But she came on the campus charter, so if she stays, she won't have a ride back. I was hoping maybe she could hitch one with us."

McGraw gives me a hesitant look, exhaling. "That's a liability, Hunter."

"I know..."

"If something happens, it falls on us. On the school."

My excitement fades. His answer settling low in the pit of my stomach. I nod my head, lowering it. "I understand."

Coach shrugs as he takes in my disappointed expression. "This goes against every school policy," he says. "But just this once, alright? You've earned some grace."

Relief floods me.

"Just this once," he repeats firmly.

I pull him into a hug before I can stop myself. "Thank you!"

He laughs, clapping my back. "She must really have you hooked."

"Yeah," I admit easily. No shame in it.

Holly owns my heart. Whether she fully realizes it yet or not.

"Well, good for you, bud." Coach says, stepping back. "You deserve something outside of basketball."

He pats my shoulder once more and walks off. I grab my shower kit, still grinning like an idiot.

After the shower and press conference, I head back to Holly. She's still on the bench where I left her, eyes drooping as she fights sleep.

God, she's cute.

I approach her quietly and tap her thigh. "Hey, baby. You ready?"

She blinks up at me, smiling as I brush her bangs from her eyes. "Yeah, sorry." She yawns as she stands. It's late and I know she's had a long day.

"It's alright." I lace my fingers through hers. "You want to go to the hotel, or do you want to go out and celebrate?"

Some of the guys —who are of age that is—are going to a bar near the hotel and invited me if I wanted to join. If Holly weren't here, I'd already be going. But now?

"It's your day," she says softly. "How do you want to celebrate?"

That answer comes really easy.

"Let's go back to hotel. Maybe order room service. Relax. We've an early bus ride tomorrow morning."

"We?" She asks, brows lifting.

"Yeah. I talked to Coach. He said you can ride back with us."

Her cheeks turn pink. "Wow. That's really nice of him. You won't get in trouble?"

"Nah," I wave it off, squeezing her hand as I guide her to the transport bay where our charter bus waits. Jalen spots us immediately.

"What up?" he claps my hand, then grins at Holly. "Holly girl, you made it!"

"I did. Apparently, Hunter can be... persuasive."

Jalen laughs loud enough to echo. We climb onto the bus and slide into seats near the middle. Holly and I sit together. Jalen drops into the seat across the aisle.

"So," he says, waggling his brows, "you two celebrating tonight?"

Holly flushes instantly. "Um... I—"

"I asked her to stay," I cut in.

Jalen gives me a slow, knowing nod. "Of course you did."

The rest of the ride passes in tired, satisfied silence.

When the bus pulls into to the hotel's valet lane, the coach stands at the front. "Alright, listen up. You've got some free time. Be smart. No shenanigans. No illegal shit, guys." He points around at all of us. "We meet back here at 6:45 AM for a seven o'clock departure. Don't do anything stupid."

A chorus of tired laughs answers him as we step off the bus.

I help Holly down, keeping her hand in mine as we head into the Omni. It's nicer than most places we stay—sleek, modern, polished.

The luxurious yet modern feel of the lobby passes by us as I bring Holly straight to the elevators and press "16". The doors slide shut.

And it's just us. The silence thickens instantly.

It takes everything in me not to pull her against the wall right there. The air between us hums, charged and heavy. I can smell her faint vanilla scent beneath the lingering smell of pretzels and arena beer.

My foot taps against the floor.

Breathe.

Slow.

Control it.

The elevator dings.

When the doors open, I dart to the left and head down the hallway toward my room. I'm extremely grateful that I don't have a roommate this trip.

Perks of being the "star", I guess.

I don't love that label. I wouldn't be anything without my team. But tonight? I'm not arguing with the benefit.

Usually, I bunk with Jalen. Sometimes Benny or Drake if the rooms are tight. We're used to it.

I reach my door, slide the key card from my wallet, and swipe. With a click, the light turns green and I push the door in. I nudge Holly inside, follow her in, and shut the door behind us, locking it. I lean back against it. And just look at her.

Her cheeks are flushed. Those honey-colored eyes—flecked with green—stare at me through her round glasses. She's wearing my jersey, paired with tiny jean shorts that show off every inch of her soft legs.

She bites her bottom lip, nervous. But not pulling away. Her gaze is warm, heated.

She inhales softly. "I'm just realizing I don't have any other clothes. I wasn't planning to stay overnight."

A chuckle slips out of me. "You don't need clothes, baby," I say quietly. "I've got everything you need."

CHAPTER 28

Holly

I SWALLOW AS HUNTER'S gaze darkens and he starts toward me.

I don't move, I can't. I have to crane my neck just to keep looking at him. He lifts a hand to my face, brushing his thumb along my cheek before tucking a loose strand of hair behind my ear.

"Have I told you how beautiful you are?" he whispers.

"Not today," I murmur, my voice betraying my nerves. I don't know why he still makes me this shaky. Butterflies riot inside my stomach.

His hands settle on my waist, guiding me backward into the room.

"You're beautiful," he breathes against my ear.

The backs of my legs hit the edge of the mattress, and I sink onto the bed. He lowers himself, slowly, sensually, kneeling in front of me without breaking eye contact. He gives me a soft kiss on my lips. "You're beautiful."

His fingers pull at the hem of my jersey, gently lifting over my head. I inhale sharply as he tosses it aside.

"You're beautiful," he murmurs again, his lips trailing along my neck, warm and soft against my skin. My head tips to the side as I close my eyes. Hunter continues to leave soft kisses on my shoulder, and then down the line of my collarbone.

He pauses over my heartbeat. "You're so fucking beautiful, Holly."

When I look at him, his expression steals the air from my lungs. No one has ever looked at me the way he does. It's not just hunger or desire. It's pure adoration.

Carefully, he slides my glasses from my face and sets them on the nightstand. Then, he stretches his body over mine, easing me back against the bed.

Somewhere between soft kisses and wandering hands, he manages to pull my shorts down. I'm left in my bra and panties, my pulse thumping. Hunter takes his time looking at me, his lips parted slightly, eyes dark as if I'm a feast.

Still kneeling over me, he pulls his shirt over his head, revealing those lean washboard abs. I reach for him instinctively, sliding my hand across his chest. The feel of every ridge and muscle beneath my palm is intoxicating. How his skin is soft with all those muscles is beyond me. My fingers drift lower feeling the small dark line of hair beneath his belly button.

Hunter catches my wrist gently.

I glance up, confused.

But instead of stopping me, he guides my hand on the outside of his sweatpants. To the erection hiding beneath. My breath stutters.

"You do this to me, Holly," he croons as he guides my hand while I stroke him. "When I think of you. When I talk to you. When I see you. This is what you do to me." Hunter then brings my hand beneath the band of his sweatpants and inside his underwear. When I feel his warmth, my lips part. He's big, and so hard. My eyes close automatically as I feel the heat beneath my palm. He is aching for me, and I ache for him.

"That's it, baby," he groans softly. "Feel what you do to me. It's all yours."

My hands grip his entire length, firm and slow. I go slow at first, looking at his face shift with every stroke. I don't have much experience with this. Just the moments I've had with Hunter. I almost feel incompetent in pleasing him with my hands or mouth alone. But I try, even if not perfectly. I want to make him feel good. I want him to feel chosen. So, I stroke his cock, learning its soft grooves and veins.

He lets me set the pace for a second before taking over, his confidence in me steadying my nerves.

"Keep going, baby girl." He commands as he removes his hand from my wrist and slips it beneath my panties. Two fingers slide between my folds, which is already slick with arousal. The first brush of those fingers pulls a helpless sound from my throat.

Applying gentle pressure on him, I focus hard on pleasing him, my body shuddering from just his fingers brushing inside my panties. Pleasure sparks everywhere at once, bright and overwhelming. We move together like that—touch for touch, breath for breath—until I'm trembling beneath him.

When he inserts those two fingers, I gasp, my back arches and my hand loses its rhythm. Hunter crashes his mouth on mine, swallowing the sound. His tongue strokes lazily against mine. His control contrasts heavily with the way my body unravels beneath him. I'm unable to continue pumping him while being pleased and kissed out of my senses. Holy shit, my body feels alive.

"Hunter!" I moan in his mouth.

As if the sound of his name flips a switch within him. In a blink, Hunter and I are naked, the rest of our clothing thrown off in a frenzy. He takes care of the condom, without taking his eyes off me. The next seconds blur, as he thrusts himself fully into me. My mouth opens wide in a silent moan; the sound stuck in my throat.

Hunter cups my chin gently, holding my face up as I look at him.

"That's it baby, let your tight pussy adjust." He thrusts harder this time. "Fuck, you take me so well."

I'm so full, I don't think I can take anymore. But then he begins moving his hips and I feel every ridge of him inside me. As he pulls and pushes into me, every inch of my skin ignites. The stretch, the heat, the closeness—it's overwhelming in the best way possible. Every motion draws another gasp from me.

Hunter's mouth moves to one of my nipples, nipping it with his teeth. I gasp. He wraps his arms around my body, holding me close to him as he continues to lazily pump into me. His breath along the nape of my neck sends goosebumps down my spine. My fingers dig into the muscles of his back, and I wrap my legs around his waist, adjusting to feel him even deeper.

"Fuck, Holly," Hunter rasps as he picks up the pace. He writhes above me, like he can't get enough of the chase he's feeling. Like he can't get enough of me. I close my eyes and enjoy every thrust, every pump, every bit of his skin that's touching me. And as the wave of my orgasm crests, Hunter follows right behind.

His face hovers above mine, our breaths still uneven as we come down. Hunter is still inside me, semi-hard, but he doesn't move. Instead, he rests his head on my chest, listening to the steady rhythm of my heart. I thread my fingers through his hair, letting the silky strands slip between them.

We lie there in silent comfort. His long limbs drape heavy over me, but I don't mind. There's something grounding about his weight, about the way I fit against him. A calm settles into my bones. It feels like something inside me has finally clicked into place. Like a missing piece found its match.

Sleep tugs at me as the room falls completely silent. When I glance at him, his eyes are closed, his breathing deep and even. He's already asleep.

I smile. Even now, there's that boyish softness to him. He looks peaceful and happy.

Carefully, I ease myself out from beneath him, moving as slow as possible so I don't wake him.

After a quick trip to the bathroom to clean up and splash water on my face, I return to find him sprawled across the bed, face down, that muscular ass in the air.

I take a moment to just look at him, hoping to never forget this image of Hunter Jace. My Hunter Jace.

I pull the sheets up and over him as best I can, then crawl back into bed beside him. Within minutes, I'm asleep too.

CHAPTER 29

Holly

"So?" Brandy slides up to the library reception desk and leans over it, chin in her hands, bright blue eyes sparkling with mischief. "How was it?" She arches a brow. I give her a look that makes her grin wider. "That good, huh?"

"Oh my God, Brandy," I roll my eyes, heat creeping into my cheeks. "It was fine."

"The game was insane," she says thoughtfully.

"It was," I agree.

"Bet the after party was better." She winks.

I groan. "It was fine." I repeat, shuffling papers that absolutely do not need shuffling.

Brandy hops up to sit on the edge of the desk. "Come on, Holly. You know me. I'm all about that smut. Give me the deets!"

I peer at her over the top of my glasses. "We spent the night together. We were both pretty tired. He fell asleep."

She narrows her eyes, flipping her long braid over her shoulder. "Why do I feel like that's not the full story?"

I fight a smile. "Because it's not, but I'm not broadcasting my personal life. We had a nice, intimate night. That's all you're getting."

She gasps dramatically. "Oooh. The serious stare? Wow. Fine. I'll drop it." She crosses her arms. "But I'm not happy about it." A beat passes before she perks up again. "So, are you going to go to the next game?"

I shrug. "I don't know. Getting there and back isn't exactly easy. And the bus ride wasn't my favorite experience."

Going down there was overwhelming. Coming back wasn't as bad, but it was still awkward—me and an entire bus full of men. Even though Hunter let me sit by the window and kept his hand in mine most of the ride, I struggled to keep up with all the jargon and play breakdowns. Half the guys were re-watching game footage, analyzing every little thing about it. Including Hunter.

He and Jalen passed the tablet back and forth, nit-picking everything. Every misstep. Every missed opportunity. Hunter explained how they'd do full footage breakdown once they were back on campus, followed by a team meeting to go over adjustments. I hadn't realized how much work happened behind the scenes. But it made for an awkward ride home.

I didn't belong there. I felt as if I was intruding on something sacred—some post-game ritual that didn't have space for me. I know Hunter was glad I came. I'm glad I did too. Still... I think I'll watch the next one from my room.

"Have you two had any tutoring sessions lately? Is he passing Shakespeare?" Brandy asks, pulling me from my thoughts.

I shrug. "The assignments he's turned in have passed. So, he should be fine. Otherwise, he wouldn't be playing. But he still has a final exam. I'll help him study for that."

Then I tilt my head. "What about you? How's it going with... what's his name? Nash?"

Brandy groans instantly. "Ugh. Don't."

"Oh no?" I tease. "Why not?"

"He's an asshole. That's why." Her mood shifts completely, the sparkle gone and replaced with a scowl.

"Why? What's he doing?"

"He's just... I don't even know what his problem is. It's like he hates me for no reason." Her shoulders slump. "We just don't click. And I know it's a temporary thing, but it's still stressful. I've got enough shit to deal with. I don't feel like dealing with him too."

"It's only a few more weeks," I say gently. "If he wants to sink, let him. You've done your part."

She exhales. "I know. I just wish I had your luck."

I laugh. "I'm still not quite sure how any of this happened."

She stands off the desk and heads toward the back offices. "Well, maybe some of that meet-cute juju will rub off on me. I wouldn't mind a sexy, broody athlete."

I shake my head as she disappears down the hall. Thankfully, my shift is almost over. And I have a date with a caramel latte at the Nest.

I scribble a pointless to-do list—mostly to look busy—and start packing up. Just as I step out from behind the desk, Hunter strides in. In all his sexy glory.

I blink with surprise. I thought he had practice.

"Hey, Hot Shot," I call when he catches my eye. "What are you doing here?"

"Thought I'd surprise my girl." He leans over the reception desk and presses a quick kiss to my lips. My cheeks instantly flush.

"Don't you have practice?" I ask as I make my way around the desk. I notice Brandy coming out to take over her shift. When she sees Hunter, she smirks.

"It's in an hour. I have plenty of time to buy my girl a latte and still make it." He slides an arm around my shoulders.

"Well, that's sweet," Brandy sings as she approaches the desk. Her eyes flick between us. "Anything urgent you need to tell me?" She glances my way.

When I shake my head, she shoos me away. "Then go clock out. Get your coffee. I've got this."

"Thanks." I hurry to the back office to clock out before anyone can stop me. The library is quiet now, but finals are coming. It won't stay that way for long.

When I return, Hunter's still there, chatting easily with Brandy. He flashes me that dazzling, all-American smile the second he sees me.

"Alright, you two have fun!" Brandy calls with a wink as we head out.

The spring sun is dipping low as we cross the Quad. A few students still linger on the grass. A couple of guys toss a Frisbee but pause when they notice Hunter walking beside me. I'm still adjusting to the looks, but I don't like the attention. My grip tightens in his hand. He notices

Instead of holding my hand, he slips his arm around me, pulling me close to his side. The gesture steadies me instantly. I haven't seen Hunter since we got back from Nashville. Sunday disappeared in homework. Then today, between classes, work and his practice schedule, I didn't think I'd see him.

So, I savor this brief time pressed against him as we make our way to the Nest. We cross Bridge Street and head toward the café. He opens the door for me, and the scent of freshly brewed coffee wraps around me like comfort. It's an instant balm to my soul.

We step up to the counter, and Hunter settles behind me, arms loosely circling my waist.

"I'll have a medium caramel latte please." I tell the barista. Then I glance back at him. "What about you, Hunter?"

"A large iced green tea with orange zest," Hunter says. "Thanks."

Before I can even reach for my wallet, he hands her a twenty. "Keep the change."

She tries to give him back. He just shakes his head.

We head to a small round table in the corner. Hunter pulls out my chair, and I sit, sliding my laptop from my bag more out of habit than intention. He takes the seat across from me.

"So," I ask. "How's your Shakespeare class going?"

"Okay," he says. "I'm passing. Thanks to you." He nudges my hand with his.

I smile. "I think you would've passed without me. You're smart, Hunter. You just needed to focus."

He lets out a low chuckle. "Maybe. But your tutoring pushed me over the edge." His gaze turns warm. "I'll always need your help, baby."

Heat creeps up my neck. "You're giving me too much credit."

"Caramel latte and green tea with orange!" the barista calls.

Still grinning, he gets up and grabs our drinks. He sets mine in front of me before sitting back down.

I take a slow sip. My eyes flutter closed as warmth spreads through me. Sweet. Familiar. Perfect as always.

When I open my eyes, he's staring at me. Smirking.

"What?" I ask.

"You don't give yourself enough credit," he says quietly. "You're incredible, Holly. You're beautiful, smart, funny, clever. You don't see half of what everyone else does."

He reaches across the table and brushes a lock of hair behind my ear, his thumb lingering along my jaw and then catching my bottom lip. My heartbeat quickens from the sensual touch.

Then he pulls back, glancing at his watch. "I have to run," he says. "Practice." He stands grabbing his tea. "But you think about what I said. And maybe later, I'll come over and remind you again." He bends down and kisses me softly. And then he's gone.

I sit there for a moment, dazed, watching him walk out of the café. It's only when the door swings shut behind him that I realize how deep I'm in.

Hunter Jace isn't just my boyfriend. He's becoming my everything.

CHAPTER 30

Hunter

THE WEEK HAS BEEN nothing but schoolwork and preparation for the next game. Elite Eight. It still feels unreal. But the grind is catching up to me.

I stand at the line, ball in hand, practicing free throws. Normally it's automatic—dribble, breathe, shoot. But tonight, my chest feels tight. Like the air won't settle.

I bounce the ball again. Focus.

The squeak of sneakers across the court sounds like nails on a chalkboard. My vision flickers at the edges.

Heat spreads across my skin. A clammy sweat forms on my brow. Something's wrong.

I step back, drawing in a ragged breath, and look toward Coach Trent.

"'Sup, Hunt?" he calls, thick brows scrunched together as he walks over.

I tuck the ball under my arm. "I'm sorry Coach, I... I don't know if I can keep going." I speak under my breath.

He studies me. "You alright? Whatcha feelin' man?"

My lungs stutter. "It's...my HCM."

His expression shifts immediately. "Alright, alright." He guides me toward the bench, steady but calm. "Sit down. What do you need?"

"Water." I swallow hard. "Rest." The word tastes like failure. "I don't want to let the team down." I press my towel to my face, trying to hide the frustration burning beneath my skin.

"Hey, hey." Coach Trent crouches in front of me. "You ain't lettin' anyone down. Alright?"

I nod, but it feels hollow.

"You're one of the hardest workers in the gym. You don't need to prove a damn thing." He squeezes my shoulder. "Go home. Get your rest. We need you healthy on Saturday."

Healthy. The word hits harder than anything else.

"Sorry, Coach."

"Don't apologize." His voice turns firm. "Your health comes first. Always. You know your body better than anyone. Take care of it, alright."

I nod again and push myself to my feet. The walk to the locker room feels longer than usual. Once inside, I slam my fist against the metal locker. Pain shoots through my knuckles.

It doesn't help. Doesn't fix anything.

Disappointment grates down on me. My shoulders feel heavy. I close my eyes and lean my head against my locker, taking deep breaths in through my nose and out through my mouth.

I drop onto the bench and drag my phone from my bag. Dozens of notifications flood the screen—emails, texts, missed calls... but I only focus on one thing. One person. I scroll to her name and start typing.

What are you up to, Stacks?

I stare at my phone, waiting for a reply. When I see the three little dots appear, a wave of relief floods over me.

Just finishing dinner. Why?

You mind coming to my dorm? I'll be there in ten.

What about practice?

I type, then delete, then type again.

I swallow hard. She asked for honesty. And she deserves it.

I don't have it in me...

The typing dots appear. Disappear. Then they reappear.

I'm on my way.

Relief loosens something tight in my chest. I grab my backpack, pull on my hoodie, and slip out of the arena. The walk back to my dorm feels harder than usual.

I sit on the steps outside, elbows braced on my knees, head hanging.

Breathe in. Out.

The air feels thinner than it should.

There's a chill settling in with the sunset, but sweat still clings to my skin. My pulse skips, then pounds, then flutters again. Wrong. It feels wrong.

For a second, I wonder if I should go to the ER. I don't want to. But if this doesn't settle... My thoughts spiral. My breaths turn shallow.

A hand rests gently on my shoulder.

I look up. Holly.

"Hey," she says softly, fingers sliding through my hair.

I don't even think. I just pull her against me, resting my head on her shoulder.

"You okay?" she whispers.

"I don't know." The words scrape on the way out. My eyes burn. I blink hard, refusing to let it break me.

She cups my face and lifts it so I have to look at her.

"What do you need?" Her voice is calm and sincere.

"You," I breathe. "Just you, baby."

She studies me for half a second, concern flickering behind her glasses, then smooths her fingers through my hair again. It elicits shivers down my spine.

"Okay," she says gently. "Let's get you inside."

I nod and push to my feet. My legs feel heavier than they should. We head into the dorm. I scan my ID and lead her toward the stairwell. Each step feels steeper than usual. My lungs lag behind my body. Air's in, but not enough.

Holly stays close, one hand steady at my back as we climb. "Easy," she murmurs. I focus on her voice.

Once we're inside my room, I lock the door and drop onto the bed. It feels like my body just gave out. Like something holding me upright finally snapped. Holly sits beside me immediately, worry written all over her face.

"Hunter, what do you need me to do?" she asks. "Is there medication you're supposed to take? Do we need to go to the hospital?"

I flex my jaw before answering. "I take something. Metoprolol. It's a beta blocker. Slows my heart rate. Takes the pressure off."

"Okay," she nods quickly. "Are you supposed to take it every day? Where is it?"

I look away. "I'm supposed to."

Her voice strains. "Supposed to?"

I exhale slowly. "Some days it makes me feel like I'm moving through mud. Slows me down. Messes with my timing on the court." I swallow. "So, sometimes I skip it. Before big practices. Or games."

Silence. When I look back at her, her eyes are wide, lips pressed thin. "Hunter," she says carefully, "that could kill you." She's so serious I can't help but chuckle tiredly.

"I know," I admit.

"Then why risk it?" Her hands curl into a fist in her lap.

I stare at the ceiling. "Because if I slow down... if I admit that I'm sick... I'm afraid they won't let me play anymore." My voice drops. "Hypertrophic Cardiomyopathy isn't exactly a selling point." The words hang between us. "I don't want them seeing me as fragile. Or replaceable."

Her expression softens. She scoots closer to me and places her palm over my chest, right above my heart. "Hunter," she says quietly, "you're not just your stats. Or your minutes. Or your seed ranking." She grazes her hand over my heartbeat. "Basketball might be where your heart is. But it's not the only thing that makes it beat."

I sit up, tension tightening my shoulders. Her hand slides down to rest on my leg.

"What else is there?" I mutter.

"You," she says, her voice soft as a feather. "Just... you. The guy who buys me my favorite drink. The one who takes me to the bookstore and pretend he's not bored. The guy who texts me just to make me smile. The one who carries his team on his back—even when he's hurting." Her voice wavers. "The guy I—"

She stops, shaking her head gently. "The guy I care about deeply. The one who has brought some purpose into my life."

Her words undo me. A small grin tugs at my mouth.

"I don't know what I did to deserve you."

She scoffs gently. "You don't earn me, Hunter. I'm not here for what you can do. I'm here for who you are." Her words land deep into my soul.

I squeeze her hand and lean my forehead against hers, breathing in her warm vanilla scent.

"Have I told you that I love you?" I whisper against her ear. Her breath catches.

"No."

I cup her face and tilt it up so I can look into her eyes. "I love you, Holly Lange. And I think I'll love you for as long as I'm alive."

Her honey-hazel eyes shimmer. "Really?" she asks, barely audible.

"Really, baby." I lean in and capture her lips with mine. It's sweet and gentle and I just want it to last forever. She tastes faintly sweet, like caramel and warmth. Threading my fingers in her hair, I deepen the kiss and explore her mouth with my tongue. I memorize the way she fits against me.

When I pull back, I keep my eyes closed for a second. I want to bask in this moment, just a bit longer. Her fingers trace along my jaw and into my hair. "I want that to be a long life," she whispers. "So, tell me where your medicine is."

A soft huff of laughter leaves me. "Nightstand drawer."

She presses a quick kiss to the corner of my mouth before reaching for it. She hands me the pill and the water she'd already grabbed.

I take it without hesitation.

"Rest," she says. "I'm right here."

I stretch back onto the bed and pull her into my arms. This time, when sleep comes, it brings peace.

CHAPTER 31

Holly

IT'S GAME DAY, AND the campus is vibrating as usual. Westbridge is hosting a viewing party in the arena for the students who couldn't make the trip. There was another charter bus heading to Nashville this morning. I didn't go.

As grateful as I was to be there last time, it was sensory overload. And I don't want to distract Hunter—not today.

They'll need everything they've got today.

Their opponent? UConn. Big. Bad. Reigning champions, UConn.

At least, that's what campus chatter says. I don't know much about them beyond what Hunter has told me. After dinner, I head back to my dorm, ready to settle in and stream the game, because I have no intention of going to Hawks Arena for the school-hosted viewing party.

The second I close my door, I swap into the Hunter's oversized sweatshirt that is now mine. Maybe it'll bring some luck.

I toss a bag of popcorn into the tiny microwave above my mini fridge, then sink into my Moon Pod chair by the bookshelf. Laptop balanced on my knees, I pull up the live-stream.

The camera pans across the Bridgestone Arena. It looks even more packed than last time. The only difference is that a sea of UConn blue drowns the Westbridge navy and gold. It doesn't surprise me. UConn is probably triple the size of our school. I curl my legs beneath me and wait.

"Welcome back to Bridgestone Arena in Nashville," the announcer says. "We're moments away from tip-off in this Elite Eight showdown between the No. 3 seed Westbridge Hawks and the perennial powerhouse, the No. 1 seed UConn Huskies."

The second announcer jumps in as the camera cuts to warm-ups. "This one has all the makings of a March classic, Mike. UConn brings its experience, depth, and that signature tournament poise. But don't count Westbridge out! This Cinderella squad has heart, hustle and they've been playing with a chip on their shoulder all season."

"No kidding," Mike continues. "The Hawks are led by their big man in the middle, Hunter Jace. He's been a force in the paint and a vocal leader on both ends. If he shows up like he did against Baylor, UConn could be in trouble."

"Jace is a matchup nightmare," the second announcer laughs. "But don't overlook the backcourt.

Jalen Carter and Benjamin West have been electric. If they're hot from deep, this game could swing fast."

"Let's not forget that this is uncharted territory for Westbridge. It's their first Elite Eight appearance in program history. The nerves will be real. But that underdog energy? That's dangerous!"

"Absolutely! David vs. Goliath tonight," the other laughs. "And Westbridge looks ready to sling some stones. Buckle up, folks! Tip-off's coming your way after the break. Don't go anywhere."

The screen cuts to commercials. My pulse is already racing. It's just commentary, but it feels bigger than that. He's bigger than that. I grab my phone and open our text thread.

Best of luck, Hunt.

I know he probably won't see it until later, but I send it anyway. I can only imagine how nervous they're feeling.

The broadcast returns. Player introductions echo through the arena. Hunter jogs onto the court, calm and locked in as the crowd erupts in cheers. He looks steady, unshaken.

My phone lights up and I peek at it.

Thanks, baby. Love you.

My breath catches. He loves me.

I couldn't believe it when he said it. I'd just stared at him like an idiot, letting the words settle instead of saying them back. I don't even know why. I've felt it for weeks. But I froze.

I don't text him back now. He won't see it anyway. I'll tell him after the game. I'm sure he'd call.

The camera shifts back to center court. Hunter lines up across from UConn's center— massive, nearly as tall as him. The ref tosses the ball up. Hunter tips it clean to Jalen. The game begins.

It's fast. Faster than any games I've watched him play. UConn moves the ball with ruthless efficiency—driving hard, finishing in the paint, crashing the boards like they're on a mission. They rebound everything. Dunk with authority.

Westbridge looks rattled, frustrated even. Hunter's jaw is tight, sweat pouring down his face. The whole team looks winded, a step slower than UConn's relentless tempo.

Ten minutes in:

WESTBRIDGE: 16 UCONN: 25

It hurts to see. Coach calls a timeout, and the screen cuts to commercial. I exhale, sinking back into my chair.

Please let whatever he says light a fire under them.

When the broadcast returns, the sportscasters break down potential adjustments. I try to follow along, but most of it flies over my head.

The game resumes.

The ref hands Jalen the ball from out-of-bounds and he passes it successfully to Benny. The guys swing the ball around, searching for an opening. UConn's defense is tight, suffocating.

Through the screen, I hear our guys shouting. Hunter's voice carries above the rest—deep, commanding, and ferocious. The kind of voice that makes my toes curl.

I almost miss the shot—

Drake pulls up from deep.

Swish. It's a three.

The crowd erupts in cheers.

UConn answers immediately, pushing the pace again. But a sloppy step sends the ball skidding loose. Jalen scoops it up and streaks downcourt.

Dunk. Another two points.

The next stretch is a tug-of-war. Westbridge slows the tempo, forcing UConn to grind for every possession instead of running them over. I barely breathe as the clock ticks down, every rebound, every pass feeling monumental.

When the buzzer blows to mark halftime, the score lights up with:

WESTBRIDGE: 31 UCONN: 38

Seven points. Not impossible.

Both teams disappear into their locker rooms as the halftime show begins. Some country star takes the stage—makes sense for Nashville—but I don't recognize her. She sang a couple songs before the sportscasters return with their halftime analysis.

None of it sounds hopeful. It'd be nice if they were at least a little impartial. I slip down the hall for a quick bathroom break before the second half starts. When I return to my room, tip-off is already underway.

Hunter looks different now. Focused. Locked in. Brows drawn tight. Jaw set. Eyes tracking the ball.

The ref tosses it up. Hunter tips it clean and the second half explodes into motion.

It's more physical this time. Harder. Hands everywhere. Elbows flying. Whistles cutting through the noise.

I hate every foul called on Hunter. I hate watching defenders crowd him, lean into him, or double up on him simply because he's bigger and better.

With his heart condition, every hit makes my stomach twist.

I'll never forget the first game I watched—where he just dropped. It's etched into my brain permanently and still makes me feel sick when I think about it.

He dominates at the free-throw line, though. He makes every shot. Despite the hard hits, he doesn't seem fazed at all. He remains focused. I'm really proud of him.

But UConn doesn't let up. No matter how hard Westbridge fights, the gap won't close. Tension spills over at one point—players shoving, voices raised—before the refs step in and call offsetting fouls.

It's brutal. Intense.

By the time the final buzzer sounds, the scoreboard flashes:

WESTBRIDGE: 68 UCONN: 82

It's over. It's not pretty. But they fought. *Hunter* fought.

He keeps his head high as he shakes hands with UConn's players and coaches, then walks toward the locker room with the rest of the team.

I close my laptop. I don't need to see anything else.

CHAPTER 32

Holly

IT'S 11:45 PM. THE game ended almost an hour ago, and I'm sitting at my desk trying to work on my English Lit paper. The screen is blank. The assignment isn't. There are dozens of authors I could choose from. I already wrote about Jane Austen—my favorite—but doing it again feels lazy, a bit redundant.

I sigh as I stare at the screen, thinking of other British authors I enjoy. Emily Brontë. Mary Shelley. Virginia Woolf. My thoughts wander. And the page stays empty. Maybe late Saturday night isn't the best time to start a paper. Especially after a loss. I tap my fingers against the desk, exhaling.

My phone buzzes violently against the wood, making me jump. When I peek at it, Hunter's name lights up. I smile and answer, putting him on speaker.

"Hey," I say softly. "How are you?"

"I'm good, baby. Tired, but good. Happy to be on the bus heading home."

He sounds exhausted. His voice is low, raspy around the edges. It makes something in my chest ache.

"So, you'll be back late?" I ask.

"Yeah." A pause. "I'd love to see you, though."

I huff a quiet laugh, "I don't know if I'll even be awake."

"Maybe just leave your door unlocked," he teases. "I'll sneak into Meadowbrooke."

I laugh outright. "Hunter, that's horrifying. How exactly would you break into an all-girls dorm?" I then add quickly, "plus, I don't want to keep my door unlocked."

"Relax," he says, amused. "No one's coming to get you except me." There's warmth beneath the joke. "I'll see you later," he adds.

The line clicks dead. I stare at my phone. Was he kidding? Would he really try to sneak? My gaze drifts to my door. Our campus is pretty safe. Nothing ever happens here.

Still.

I groan. I'm ridiculous. But I stand and unlock it anyway. I'm a lovesick fool.

I shut my laptop off—this paper isn't happening tonight—and grab my book instead. Curling onto my bed beneath the dim glow of my lamp, I try to read. I don't make it past a few pages before sleep takes me.

My door clicks softly, and I stir. My heart jumps when I see his silhouette crossing the room.

"Hey, baby," Hunter whispers, pressing a kiss to my temple.

"Hey," I breathe, still half-asleep. I close my book which has fallen to the wayside and set it on the nightstand. He strips down to his boxer briefs and crawls into bed with me. His cologne wraps around me instantly—familiar, intoxicating. It makes my core twitch, even when I'm sleepy. He nuzzles into my neck.

"Hunter..." I whisper-moan.

"You're wearing my sweatshirt," he groans when his hand slips beneath it. He sucks in a breath when his hand reaches my bare breasts. "With nothing underneath. Shit. Holly, is this what you wore all night? I'd rather have been here." When he chuckles, his breath hits my neck and goosebumps rise all over my skin.

"I was wishing you luck," I admit. He squeezes me against his almost-naked body, and I can feel his erection growing between my thighs.

"Fuck, Holly," he mutters. "I just wanted to sleep. But now I'm feeling wired." His hands roam over my skin, touching each bare inch he can find. The sensation lights up every nerve within me.

"You should rest," I whisper. "That was a hard game." I don't know who I'm trying to convince—him or me—because honestly, I want him.

"It was," he agrees. Then his voice drops. "But baby... you feel too good right now." He kisses me and my world tips. I'm fully awake and horny now. I shift, rolling him onto his back and swing a leg over him. His hardness hits me between my thighs and instinctively, I rub myself against him.

His eyes light up as he smirks. "Damn, Hols," he murmurs, his hands sliding to my hips. "Aren't you needy tonight?"

I press a hand to his chest, holding him in place. "I'm not fucking needy. A tall, sexy man broke into my room and has turned me on. Now, I'm a horny mess."

His dick twitches as his gaze darkens. "Then take it," he rumbles beneath me.

I slide my panties off before ripping his boxers from his body. All at once, I spear myself on him; a loud moan escaping my throat as I take him in. It's overwhelming. He's overwhelming. In the best way possible.

I feel the sting as my body stretches to accommodate him. I still for a moment, adjusting, and grounding myself in the feel of him beneath me. His hands tighten on my thighs as he exhales curses under his breaths.

Once I steady my breathing, I begin to move my hips, back and forth. Slow at first. The friction builds, warm and addictive, and I lean into it—chasing how it makes my head spin. Hunter doesn't interrupt. He simply watches from below, as if in awe. That look alone makes me bolder. I lose myself as I writhe on him; my body buzzing as I quicken my pace.

His hands find my hips, fingers digging in as our pace syncs. Every shift of my body pulls a rough sound from him, and it fuels me. I want to unravel like this. I want to take him with me. I groan as the muscles in my core tighten, squeezing around him as I ride him with everything I have.

I brace my palms against his muscular chest. My body begins to spasm. I know I'm close to an orgasm. My control slips, my muscles tighten, but Hunter has me. His grip firms, guiding the rhythm when mine falters.

The pleasure crests fast and fierce, pulling a moan from my throat as everything inside me releases at once. Hunter follows right behind while my core clutches him. His sensual lips form an "o" as he comes. I feel him throbbing inside me, and it's sexy and fulfilling, all at once.

For a moment, neither of us moves. I lean forward, resting my hand over his heart. It's racing. His eyes stay closed as he exhales slowly. "Fuck, baby. Where did *this* Holly come from?"

"I don't know," I admit. "Maybe this Holly comes out when she's woken and fondled in the middle of the night."

He pulls me down against him, arms locking around my waist. "Maybe I should do it more often then."

He presses his lips on mine, dragging it out, nibbling on my lips.

"I'm not even going to ask how you managed to sneak in," I whisper between breathless kisses.

He grins, "Good, I wouldn't tell you anyway. It's my little secret."

We settle onto our sides, facing each other. The room is quiet now, the earlier heat replaced with something softer.

"Seriously though," I say gently, brushing my fingers along his jaw. "How are you feeling? About the game."

He shrugs. "We knew it was a long shot. Am I disappointed? Yeah. But, it's okay. We still made it to the Elite Eight. It's the farthest in Westbridge's basketball program." His mouth curves slightly. "I'm proud of that."

"I'm proud of you," I whisper running my hand through his mussed up hair. It's grown out since we met; I notice a slight curl at the ends. "You've overcome so much... and the public doesn't even know."

"They don't need to," he says, his voice dropping. "The less they know, the better. I want to keep my private life private."

I nod, though a knot forms in my chest. "That makes sense."

His thumb brushes my lower lip, sensing my shift. "Not you, baby... if that's what you're thinking."

I look into his eyes.

"I want the world to see you." He kisses me, pulling my face toward his with both his hands.

"That's sweet, but not necessary," I whisper against his lips. "Besides, if you get drafted to the NBA, where does that leave me? I still have a year left here. You'll have a whole career ahead of you, Hunter."

The mood shifts, turning heavy.

"What are you saying, Holly? You think this is a fling? That I'm going to leave you behind once I graduate?" His brows knit together, his jaw setting into a hard line.

"I don't know," I admit. "I don't know what the future holds."

"I do." He pushes onto his elbow, hovering over me, until I'm pinned against the mattress. "It involves you and me. Everything else is just noise. I love you, Holly. That's not changing. Not in a few days. Not in a few weeks. Not after graduation, and not after the draft. You're in my court, and you're my endgame."

I stop breathing, the words vibrating through me. "In your court?"

"Yeah." He kisses me again, lingering this time. "And I want you to stay there forever."

CHAPTER 33

Holly

THE FINAL WEEKS OF the semester pass in a blur. Since their elimination from March Madness, Hunter has been swept into a whirlwind of interviews, sports podcasts, and scouts. My own world has been buried under a mountain of library shifts and the heavy, multi-page essays that count as finals for most of my classes. Being a Literary Arts major means my GPA depends far more on papers than exams.

Hunter and I still meet weekly for tutoring, and when we can, we carve out time to be together. A quiet night here or there. Sometimes a late-night coffee at the Nest or an early breakfast before class. Even with basketball season over, we seem busier than ever. I had hoped for more time together. More peace. Especially now that it feels like our time is running out.

He says we'll outlast whatever obstacles come our way, and I know he means it. I believe everything he says about us. But can I really let myself believe he won't forget about me when basketball takes him to Toronto or Minnesota? Wherever he's drafted, he'll have to move. What then? Long distance? FaceTime calls a few nights a week?

The thoughts make me nauseous, like I've stepped in too deep. I've fallen head over heels for Hunter, and now that I have, I don't know what happens if it falls apart. *When* it falls apart.

"Hey, girl!"

Brandy's voice startles me at my table, where I'd been pretending to study before getting lost in my thoughts.

"Whoa, sorry. didn't mean to scare you."

"It's okay," I say. "Just thinking."

"Good thoughts, I hope?" She asks, brow arching.

I huff a breath. "I don't know."

"Talk to me." Brandy brushes her sandy-blonde hair behind her ears as she takes the seat across from me. Her pale eyes narrow slightly, fingers steepling on the table. "Tell me. What's up?"

"I... I'm just... overthinking." I wave a hand like it's no big deal.

"Uh huh," she says dryly. "You're not getting away with that blasé answer, Holly. Not this time. Let me in."

I groan, rolling my eyes. "I just... what happens to Hunter and me once he graduates and gets drafted into the NBA? He'll leave with whatever team picks him up, and I'll still be here. Starting senior year. You don't think he'll eventually lose interest in a small-town girl like me? He says all these beautiful things… and I have all these… feelings…" I take a deep breath, willing myself not to cry. "Why do I feel like I'm going to be the one who gets hurt?"

She sighs, sympathy softening her face. "Oh, hun." She squeezes my hand until I look at her. "He's really got you good, huh?"

We manage a small laugh, but tears still sting my eyes. "You need to take it one day at a time, Hols. Be with him. Enjoy it. Worry about the future later. You're young and in love. Just ride with it!"

I give her a weak smile. Maybe she's right. Maybe it'll all work out. But what do I know? I don't know the future. I only have right now.

"You're right," I say quietly. "I should just enjoy being with him while I can."

Later that evening, Hunter and I sit in his dorm room, reviewing for his Shakespeare exam. A tense silence stretches between us, thick enough to make my pulse jump.

Abruptly, he pushes back from the bed and drops into the chair at his desk, staring at the papers scattered on it. I watch as he rakes a hand through his hair and bites the corner of his lip.

"I'm declaring tomorrow," he says without looking at me.

My stomach flips. This is the moment I've been dreading. I don't want to hold him back, so I force normalcy in my voice. "That's...big."

He nods, still avoiding my eyes. "Yeah. It is."

Silence settles again, heavy and unspoken. I curl in on myself, arms folding across my chest. "That happened fast. I didn't think it would be this soon."

He looks up then, his gaze finding mine the way it always does. Steady, supportive... yet searching.

"I'm really proud of you," I add quickly.

"But?"

The single word makes my heart pound. He's completely still, like he's bracing for impact.

"I just..." I shift, standing from the bed and leaning against its wooden frame. "I feel this is the part where you turn the page, and I become the chapter you outgrew when your real story starts."

His expression shifts from gentle to fierce in an instant. He closes the distance between us in one step. "You're not a chapter," he states firmly. His fingers hook under my chin, lifting my gaze to his. "You're the whole damn book."

I scoff. "Hunter... you're getting my hopes up."

I glance away, but he refuses to let me retreat. His grip tightens slightly, bringing my gaze back to his.

"This draft might change my jersey. My city. Maybe even my mindset." He leans in, close enough that I feel the heat of his breath. "But you? You're what I hold on to. You're the face I will see behind every play, every shot, every headline. Come what may."

Tears blur my vision. "You say that now. But what if you get drafted and everything changes?"

"It won't," his voice drops to a whisper. "You're in my court, remember? You're my endgame. Wins, losses, championships… none of that matters more than you. You're it for me, Holly. The biggest win of my life, baby."

The tears spill over. My lip quivers as something inside me breaks and mends all at once. I step into him, wrapping my arms around his waist and pressing my face to his chest. The warmth of him. The scent of him. Being held like this. It's my favorite place to be.

He kisses the top of my head, chin resting there as he pulls me closer. "You're stuck with me, Short-Stack. Through thick and thin. Don't you dare forget it."

CHAPTER 34

Holly

I SIT IN HAWKS Arena, surrounded by a packed crowd and the four-hundred plus students set to graduate. I'm alone in the stands, but I promised Hunter I'd be here. So, I am. He gave one ticket to me and two to his parents. He doesn't have siblings, and he said he'd introduce me to his parents after the ceremony.

That thought alone makes me nervous as hell.

I'm wearing a white floral sundress with spaghetti straps and wedges. It's a warm spring afternoon, the kind that makes everything seem possible. Some of the seniors will probably do a fountain run at Founder's Fountain once this is over. I wonder if Hunter will join them. If the basketball team will go together.

The ceremony begins—long and drawn out, something I'll have to sit through again next year. The guest speaker is decent. The valedictorian does well. Then they start calling names. Cheers and air horns echo through the arena as each graduate crosses the stage.

When Hunter's name is announced, the entire place erupts.

He walks across the stage in his navy cap and gown, cords draped around his neck. One for basketball, I assume. Maybe another for his fraternity. He looks so handsome. I clap until my palms sting as he shakes the university president's hand and accepts his diploma.

This is it. He's officially done with college. On his way to the big leagues.

Pride swells in my chest. He's overcome more than most people ever will. And he's still standing. Still fighting. I love him. Not just the athlete or the future professional. I just love everything about him. He is an amazing man. I know he's going to inspire a lot of kids in his life.

When the ceremony ends, I move with the crowd outside and wait for the graduates to filter through. I'm not sure where to stand, so I head to the bench where I waited for him after the first game I ever attended. It seems like a lifetime ago. But it's only been a few months. Being with Hunter has always been easy. In a way, it feels like we've known each other since forever.

A roar of cheers rises somewhere in the distance, and I have a feeling that it's for Hunter. There's always a crowd around him. I wait. We'll find each other. I want him to enjoy this without me hovering or clinging onto him.

All around me, graduates pose with family and friends, taking pictures, laughing, and simply enjoying the day. Flowers and balloons bob in the air. Confetti drifts across the pavement. I smile as I take it in. I tilt my face toward the sun and close my eyes, letting the warmth settle into my skin.

"Hey, gorgeous." A deep, familiar voice croons, and I open my eyes.

Hunter stands in front of me, tall enough to block the sun, light outlining his shoulders.

"Hey, Hunter." I stand, and he pulls me in for a kiss. "Congratulations. You're officially a college graduate."

"That I am."

"How does it feel?" I ask, brushing my fingers over the cords around his neck.

"Pretty good. Glad to be done, but nervous about what's next." He wraps his arm around my waist, pulling me against his side. Two middle-aged people approach from behind him, and the resemblance is immediate.

The woman is tall—easily six feet—with dark hair swept up neatly and sharp brown eyes. She wears a navy-blue dress and a thick gold chain drapes at her neck.

"Mom, this is Holly."

She steps forward and takes my hand. "Oh my, Hunter! She's adorable. Hi, Holly. I'm Lia Jace. It's so nice to finally meet you. Hunter's told me so much about you." Her voice is a lovely alto—warm and cozy.

"Really?" I glance at Hunter before smiling back at her. "That's so sweet, thank you. It's nice to meet you too."

A tall man moves beside her.

"This is my dad," Hunter says.

"I'm Thomas Jace." He offers his hand. He's at least six-foot-five, broad shouldered and composed. Salt-and-pepper hair. A neatly trimmed beard. Navy suit with gold-patterned tie. Suddenly, Hunter being six-nine makes perfect sense.

"It's a pleasure," I say, shaking his hand.

"We're heading to Barrel and Bloom for dinner," Mrs. Jace says with a hopeful smile. "We made reservations for four, if you'd like to join us."

"That's very kind. Of course, I'd love to." I glance at Hunter, who's trying not to laugh.

"Yes, Holly. I insist." He gives me a small squeeze, and I nod.

An hour later, we're seated at Barrel and Bloom, the nicest restaurant on campus. It sits on Bridge Street, beside the Nook. The place has an upscale steakhouse vibe, with exposed brick and Edison bulbs hanging from the ceiling, sepia photographs of cattle and wild plains cover the walls. I've never eaten here before—it's always been out of my budget—but I've heard it's good.

"So, Holly," Mrs. Jace says as a waiter sets down a basket of rolls, "what are you majoring in?"

I clear my throat. "Literary Arts."

"Interesting," Mr. Jace comments. "What are you hoping to do with that?"

His tone isn't unkind, just curious. Still, compared to Hunter's future, my answer suddenly feels small.

"Honestly, I'm not 100% sure yet," I admit. "I work in the library right now, and I've thought about pursuing something along those lines."

"Working in a library?" he repeats, a slight unease slipping into his voice. Heat creeps up my neck, and I'm grateful for the dim lighting.

"Dad." Hunter's tone carries a quiet warning.

"Sorry, bud. I don't mean anything by it. Just curious. I didn't realize you needed a degree to run a library."

I press my lips together, unsure how to respond.

Thankfully, Hunter's mom steps in. "Tom, that's enough." Her voice is stern, final.

"It's okay," I stutter, even though it isn't. Not entirely. "I really love reading. I've always gravitated toward British literature—Jane Austen, especially. That's what drew me into Literary Arts in the first place. I'm a bit of a bookworm." I manage a small smile. "There are a lot of paths with it. Publishing industry, or owning a bookstore. I've considered becoming an editor or a literary agent."

"If it weren't for Holly, I wouldn't have passed Shakespeare," Hunter says, pride clear in his voice.

I laugh softly. "That's not true."

"Oh, it's absolutely true," he counters, smirking. "I wasn't passing before tutoring, and I finished with a B minus. So... you can downplay it all you want, but I know the truth."

I roll my eyes, but warmth flickers in my chest.

The conversation shifts after that. I don't want to argue with him. Especially not in front of his parents.

Hunter and his parents talk about him moving him out of his dorm. The NBA combine in two weeks. Chicago. Travel plans. Evaluations. The added concern of his HCM, which he's already told them I know about. Much to his father's chagrin.

I listen, nodding when appropriate.

As they map out his future in careful detail, something inside me grows quiet. I understand his father's hesitation now. This world—the combines, the travel, the contracts—feels so far removed from mine. They talk about what's next for him. And I sit here, wondering where I fit in. For the first time all evening, I feel small. Almost invisible. Like this is the moment the page begins to turn. And, I can do nothing to stop it.

CHAPTER 35

Holly

IT'D BEEN JUST UNDER a week since graduation, and I haven't seen Hunter once.

He's called. Texted. Left voicemails. I haven't answered any of them.

After dinner with his parents, I crumbled in on myself. I made a weak excuse to leave early that night. He looked skeptical, maybe even hurt, but he let me go.

Now I think I'm doing him a favor. I can't handle the slow unraveling that's coming. The inevitable goodbye. I have to do it first... sever the thread.

My heart already feels cracked open, and I don't have it in me to face him.

I'm curled into my Moon Pod chair, a copy of *Persuasion* open in my lap. Summer classes start in two weeks. I'm not taking any, but I'll be working full-time at the library, which lets me keep my dorm room. At least, I don't have to move out. It's easier than going home.

My parents are always busy. My older brother, Jeremy, is in med school at UNC—their pride and joy. My younger sister, Lily, is finishing her sophomore year of high school. Mom teaches full-time and dad has his accountant job. Their lives are full. There's never really been space for me. So, I stay here.

I've read *Persuasion* more times than I can count, but tonight the words blur together. My gaze drifts to the window as the late spring sun dips low toward the horizon. My phone buzzes. Hunter's name flashes on the screen. I silence it. It buzzes again. I silence that one too. Then I hear the ping. A text message. Then another. I don't open them. If I read them, I might break.

My throat tightens, but I blink the tears away and force my eyes back to the page.

A sudden pounding at my door startles the shit out of me. My heart slams against my ribs as I cross the room and crack it open.

Hunter stands there, eyes wild, jaw tight. The second he sees me, he pushes the door open and steps inside, shutting it firmly behind him. His face is distraught, filled with so many emotions, I'm not sure what he's going to do.

"What are you doing here?" I ask as he paces my room like a caged animal, dragging a hand through his already disheveled hair.

"Why are you avoiding me?" he demands. "Why won't you answer your phone?"

"I—"

"Did my dad scare you off?" he cuts in before I can even gather the words. "He can be an asshole sometimes, but he just wants what's best for me. I'm sorry if he crossed a line." Hunter rambles.

"He wasn't wrong, Hunter." I say quietly, studying the floor. "I'm just a small-town girl with no real future. You… you're about to be something. You're going places I'll never see."

"Stop," he commands, prowling toward me.

I wrap my arms around myself, "I'm just trying to protect myself. I can't watch you move on and find out about it online."

"Stop it, Holly." His voice hardens as he steps right in front of me. I keep my eyes down, focusing on our feet. His fingers slide under my chin, lifting my face but I squeeze my eyes shut. I can't look at him.

"Look at me, Holly."

My lip trembles. I shake my head.

"Look at me."

"I think you should go, Hunt." I whisper.

"Don't push me away." His voice strains. "Don't do this."

I finally meet his eyes. They're wrecked. His whole face is tense, his jaw clenched. He's desperate.

"Don't make this harder than it has to be," I say, forcing the words out. The tears slip free. "You have to be in Chicago next week. You need to focus on your future. I don't want to be another distraction."

As my tears fall, I bring a hand up to his face. Brush my fingers along his jaw. There's new scruff there. I give him a weak smile, or at least try to. We stand close enough to feel each other breathe.

“This was my last-ditch effort,” he says quietly. “My parents are waiting in the car. But I just…” He stops, his breath shaky, those puppy-dog brown eyes filled with unshed tears. His hands cradle my face. “Endgame, baby,” he whispers.

He kisses me—deep, familiar, devastating. Warm tears streak down my cheeks.

When he pulls back, he doesn’t linger. Abruptly, he turns for the door.

“I’ll be rooting for you,” I manage.

He pauses only a second before walking out and closing the door behind him. The silence that follows is deafening. Unbearable.

I sink back into my chair and curl up, the book abandoned on the floor. I let myself fall apart.

CHAPTER 36

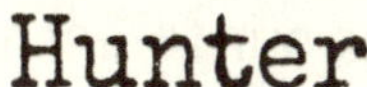

Hunter

The gym lights are blinding. Too bright.

I blink once. Twice. The glare bouncing off the hardwood burns my eyes. That's not the only reason they sting.

My parents sit front row in the stands. Mom gives me a small wave. Dad nods, supportive and proud. I nod back, jaw tight.

There's no sign of her. Not that I expected there would be.

The silence between us has been suffocating. Phantom vibrations. Real ones too. Every buzz of my phone sending a spike of hope through me before reality settles back in.

We're not broken up. I won't call it that. It's a little break. A breather. That's what I tell myself.

She said she's small-town. Said this isn't her world. That she doesn't want to hold me back. She said... a lot of things.

Every word landed like a punch.

I roll my shoulders back. Focus.

"Jace," a scout barks. "You're up."

Lane agility. Easy.

I crouch, fingertips grazing the floor. I take a deep breath.

"Go."

I explode forward. Pivot. Shuffle. Cut tight. My muscle memory takes over. I've done this drill a thousand times.

The stopwatch beeps. Scouts murmur to each other.

I don't look at them. I'm not here for their approval. The only reaction I care about isn't here.

I head toward the next drill spot. Max Vertical.

I step up, my heart pounding harder than it should.

Not nerves. Her. She's everywhere in my head. In the silence between reps. In every breath.

"Go," the next scout cues.

I jump. Higher than I ever have. I reach as far as I can, my fingertips brushing the marker at the top.

There's a sharp reaction behind me. A low curse. Pens scratching fast across paper.

My chest heaves. Not from the effort. From the ache.

But I straighten, shoulder back. If I can't have her here—I'll at least win this.

I step out of the locker room, tugging my sweatshirt over my head. My muscles still hum from the drills, in a good way. My shoes squeak against the polished floor as I walk down the hallway—away from the noise and spotlight of the combine.

"Nice work today."

I stiffen.

Dad stands near the vending machines, arms crossed. That familiar gleam in his eyes—the one that I've grown-up with. The look that means I did well, but not well enough.

"You're going first round if they've got half a brain," he says as he steps closer. "Especially after that vertical. Hunt, that was incredible."

"Thanks." I shrug. "We'll see."

There's a pause. I already know what's coming, but hope dad keeps his mouth shut.

"Now imagine if you'd stayed focused all season," he continues in his preachy tone. "No distractions. No girlfriend pulling your mind off the game, ruining your March Madness run."

My jaw clenches. "There it is," I mutter. "She wasn't a distraction."

"Son, we've been over this," he says evenly. "She was sweet, sure. But we both know she doesn't fit into this world. You've got a shot at something real. A legacy. NBA. Endorsements. Millions—"

"I don't care about millions!" The words come out sharper than I intend. "Not without her."

He goes still, his thick brows shoot up in surprise.

"She didn't care about any of this," I continue, my voice low but steady. "She showed up anyway. Learned the game. Just to support me. Not the hype. Not the name. Me."

Dad says nothing.

"She didn't want my money. Or my future contracts. She just believed in me." I swallow. "And I let her walk away because she thought she was holding me back. So yeah, Dad... let's call her a distraction."

The judgment in his eyes wavers.

"You think winning is the contract," I say. "The headlines. The money. Maybe it is to you. But doing it alone? That's not winning, Dad. Not to me."

Silence stretches between us. I shake my head and walk past him. For once, he doesn't follow.

CHAPTER 37

Holly

I SIT AT THE reception desk in Hawthorne Library, doing absolutely nothing.

The place is dead. Silent. Not a single student in sight. I'm sure they're all at Tailfeathers on Bridge Street, crowded around TVs for the NBA Draft.

Tonight could be Hunter's big night.

I open my laptop and pull up the broadcast myself. I don't really understand how the draft works—when names get called, how long it takes, what determines the order. I just know his name could be one of them.

The camera pans across New York City, lights glittering against the dark sky. Times Square. The Statue of Liberty. Then the Barclays Center, glowing.

Inside, the arena is packed. Mostly potential draft picks.

I scan the crowd, searching for one face. The lighting makes it hard to see anyone clearly. For a second, I almost laugh. Hunter has never blended into a room in his life.

Part of me wonders if he's even there. I shake the thought away. Where else would he be? This is what he's worked for. I know he's there.

We haven't spoken since the night he showed up at my dorm. I try not to think about it. Even weeks later, it still feels raw. Like something half-healed that aches if I press on it.

He is my first love. And I don't know if that's something you ever fully let go of. Sometimes, I wonder if he'll be my last love, too. The thought of starting over with someone else feels impossible. Nothing has ever felt as easy as it did with him.

On the screen, names are called one after another. I don't recognize any of them, but each player stands, emotional, shaking hands with the commissioner before slipping on a team hat.

I take a sip of my caramel latte. It's gone cold—I've been nursing it for hours. Exhaustion pulls at me, and I'm just ready for my shift to be over. The library is so quiet I can hear the hum of the air conditioning.

They're into the twenties now. The twentieth pick goes to Boston Celtics. The player wipes at his eyes as he walks to the stage, smiling wide as he puts on his new hat. I lean closer to the screen.

After a few more minutes, the commissioner steps to the podium again. "With the twenty-first pick in the 2025 NBA draft..."

The video glitches. Of course, the library connection is crapping out. I mutter a curse, heart pounding as the screen buffers. Then it snaps back into focus.

"...the Miami Heat selects Hunter Jace, center, Westbridge State University."

My breath leaves me in a rush. I'm on my feet before I realize it, hands flying to my mouth. The camera swivels, and there he is. Hunter. Dressed in a fitted black suit, standing tall, composed. He smiles—not the easy grin I know, but something steadier. Controlled.

He walks to the stage, shakes hands, accepts a Miami Heat hat, and places it on his head like he was always meant to wear it. He looks like someone the whole world is about to know.

Tears blur my vision. He did it. A broken laugh escapes me as I wipe at my cheeks. "I'm so proud of you, Hot Shot." I whisper to myself.

The broadcast cuts to his parents. His mom is crying openly. His dad claps, chest puffed with pride.

For a brief selfish second, I imagine myself beside him. Hugging him. Kissing him. Telling him how proud I am. Somehow, I can still hear his voice. *"You're in my court. You're my endgame."*

Instead, I'm here. Alone. The draft moves on, but I don't hear the next name. I choke back a sob. I feel like such a fool. But I had to let him go. For his future. For this exact moment. And still...

My gaze drops to my phone. Our message thread stares back at me. I type something. Delete it. Type again. Before I can overthink it, I hit his name and press call.

It rings. Once, twice, then a third time before going to voicemail. His voice fills my ear—calm, familiar—and it nearly undoes me. It brings back all the memories and I suppress another sob.

"Hey... I just watched you go first round. Miami." I let out a small, breathless laugh. "Of course you end up somewhere warm and sunny." There's a pause as my thoughts scatter. "I'm proud of you, Hunter. So proud I can barely breathe. You deserve this. Every second of it."

I swallow. "I know you probably don't want to hear from me. And I understand that. I just... I'm really happy you're living your dream." My voice falters. "I let mine go. That's on me." I take another pause, steadying myself. "Anyway. Congratulations."

I hang up and drop my head back with a groan. "What an idiot."

I stare at my phone, equal parts horrified and embarrassed. A pathetic, desperate rambling voicemail to a newly drafted NBA player Hunter Jace.

Fantastic.

Outside the library's glass doors, the night has settled in fully. It's nearly midnight, and my shift is almost over.

I close my laptop and began shutting everything down, the silence echoing through me. I glance across the empty rows of shelves. Is this it? Is this the version of my life I chose because it felt safe? Hunter is stepping into something bigger. And suddenly, I'm not just missing him. I'm questioning myself.

CHAPTER 38

Hunter

I PLAY THE VOICEMAIL again. Probably for the tenth time. Her voice fills the quiet hotel room, soft yet shaky. It settles something in me. Even through the distance, I can hear it—the pride. The hurt.

She's proud of me. I knew she would be. The draft night chaos fades when I listen to her. The cameras. The handshakes. The congratulations. None of it matters as much as that shaky "I'm proud of you."

I sit on the edge of the hotel bed and close my eyes. God, I miss her so fucking much. It's like a constant ache that won't let up. Holly Lange got under my skin in a way no one ever has. And I'm done pretending we're on a "break." We're not over. We're just unfinished.

Now that the draft's done, I have one job left. Fix this.

We're endgame. I know that. I wasn't the one to ever believe in soulmates, but if they exist, I know Holly's mine and I'm hers.

Tomorrow, they fly me to Miami for media, a meet-and-greet, and a facility tour. First round pick means guaranteed contract. The details will come later—years, numbers, clauses.

Everything is moving so fast. My future is secure for a little while. But none of it feels right if she's not part of it.

Summer league. Training camp. Apartment hunting. A whole new city. I want her there. And if she thinks she doesn't belong in my world. Then I'll build a new one that fits us both.

I grab my phone. Time to stop listening to voicemails. Time to go get my girl.

I stare at Holly's name on my screen. I should call her back. I want to call her back. The urge wins out.

I press her name. It rings.

And rings.

And rings.

My foot taps against the carpet.

"Hello?" Her bleary, sleep-ridden voice answers the phone. I almost cry with relief. "Hey, Short-Stack." I keep tone low.

"Hunter?" She sounds more awake now. "Is everything okay? Did you mean to call me?"

A small laugh slips out. "Yeah, I meant to call you. I got your message."

"Oh." A pause. "I'm sorry about that. I probably shouldn't have."

"I'm glad you did," I admit.

Another pause

"I just felt like a real congratulations was better than a text," she says softly. "You deserved it. I'm so proud of you." She yawns, and it wrecks me more than anything else. I don't let the silence linger.

"I miss you, Holly." The words come with certainty. "Every second of tonight, I wanted you there. I'm grateful. I'm excited. But it's not the same without you by my side."

She exhales slowly. "Hunter... we've already talked about this."

"No," I say, gently but firmly. "You told me how it had to be. That's not the same as talking."

Silence.

"I want you," I continue. "Not just when it's easy. Not just when it fits neatly into the plan. I love you. I still love you. And I'm not walking away because you're scared."

A soft sniffle comes through the line. I close my eyes. I don't want her to cry. It aches me to see her in tears.

However, for a split second, doubt creeps in. What if I'm the only one still fighting? But I push the thought back.

Silence stretches between us. I wonder if she's fallen asleep. Then she finally speaks.

"I think I ruined my life pushing you away, Hunter." Her voice shakes. "It's just... this is a lot. And now you're going to Miami. We won't be able to see each other. Maybe not at all."

"That's not true." I say, softer now. "There's an off-season. I promise basketball doesn't run twelve months a year." I let a small smile edge into my words. "Summer will be busy, yes. But after that, we'll figure it out. We will."

She doesn't respond right away.

"Don't give up on me, baby," I say. "I'm not going anywhere. Not like that."

A shaky breath comes through the line. The pause that follows feels endless. Then—

"Okay." It's barely above a whisper.

Another pause.

"I love you."

I go still. A slow smile spreads across my face as I close my eyes.

"I love you too," I say, meaning it more than anything I've ever said. "I'll call you tomorrow before I fly out. We'll take this one step at a time."

"Okay, Hunt...goodnight."

"Goodnight."

The line clicks dead. I stare at my phone for a second longer, then let out a breath I didn't realize I was holding.

Miami. Contracts. Media. Training camp. None of it feels overwhelming now. Because she's still here.

CHAPTER 39

Holly

It's the first week of August, and Westbridge State is starting to buzz again. New students moving into dorms. Upperclassmen returning. Campus feels alive again.

I'm excited for senior year.

Summer had been slow. Quiet. Long shifts at the library. I was relieved when Brandy came back—she's really my only friend here. I don't mind, though. I've always preferred a smaller circle. Mostly my own company.

After my shift, I stop at the Nest for a caramel latte. All I want is to change into pajamas and curl up with my current read.

By the time I swipe into my dorm, I'm exhausted. The walk from Bridge Street isn't far, but it feels longer tonight.

I climb the stairs, dig my key from my bag, and unlock my door.

The second I step inside, I freeze. My coffee nearly slips from my hand.

"Hunter?"

He's standing in the middle of my room, holding a bouquet of red roses. The familiar scent of his cologne hits me first. Then him.

He looks... different. The same, but sharper. Dark scruff along his jaw. Hair slightly longer, swept back. A fitted black polo with a small Miami Heat logo over his chest. Dark jeans.

He looks mature. Like a man stepping into his future.

"Hey, Holly."

He takes two steps toward me, filling the tiny space effortlessly. He hands me the roses, then reaches past me to gently close the door I'd left hanging open.

"They're stunning, thank you." I say softly, bringing them to my nose before looking back up at him. "What are you doing here? And how did you even get in?"

His gaze darkens as it sweeps over me. It sends a thrill straight through my spine.

"I'm here to see you, baby. Summer league's over. I've got a little time off." A hint of a smile curves his mouth. "As for how I got in... let's say I still have my ways."

I laugh softly, still staring at him like he might disappear. I set the roses on my desk and step back into him. My palm presses against his chest, solid and warm. I need to feel him. To make sure this isn't some cruel daydream.

"You're real?" My voice sounds so small and pathetic.

A low chuckle rumbles from him as his arms slide around my waist. "Very real, baby."

I'd watched every summer league game. Every highlight. Every post-game interview. We'd texted. Talked. But seeing him in person again—feeling him—is something else entirely.

"How's Miami?" I ask, though my pulse is too loud in my ears to focus on his answer.

"Fantastic," he says, voice low and steady. "Everything I'd dreamed of and more."

"Is that so?" I challenge lightly. "Then why are you here?"

"Because you're the more," he murmurs. "And I've been dying to kiss you since the second I walked out of this room last time."

He leans down slowly. His warm lips find mine, soft at first. Then deeper.

My eyes flutter close as I melt into him. His grip tightens slightly, like he's afraid I might slip away.

The feel of him is everything. It's all I've missed, all I've yearned for and now that he's here, with me, I don't want to let him go. I won't let him go. Not again.

I want Hunter Jace. I never knew how much I'd want him until I no longer had him. I pull back just enough to breathe. "I've missed you so much," I whisper against his lips.

A low sound escapes him. "You have no idea." His thumb traces along my jawline.

"So," I murmur, brushing my fingers down the front of his polo, "where are you staying?"

He sighs, amused. "I've got a room at the Hilton past Bridge Street." His eyes darken slightly. "So, the real question is... would you like to stay with me for a couple days? Or should I plan on squeezing into this dorm?"

I laugh softly, glancing around my tiny room. The shared bathrooms of an all-girls dorm. The paper-thin walls.

"Yeah," I say, already reaching for my overnight bag. "I think the Hilton sounds like a much better idea."

He grins. "I was hoping you'd say that."

I move around the room quickly, tossing a few essentials into my bag. He watches me like he's memorizing every movement. When I bend to pack up my pajamas, he gives me a playful smack at my butt.

I gasp, swatting his arm back. He laughs, "Ow!"

Before we leave, I tuck the roses into my oversized water bottle so they won't wilt while I'm gone. Then I slip my hand into his.

This time, I don't hesitate. I choose him. And I choose myself, too.

When we arrive at Hunter's hotel suite, I stop short. It's stunning. A luxurious king-sized bed dominates the center of the room, and glass doors open onto a balcony overlooking the Appalachian Mountains.

"Wow." I exhale, as I step out onto the balcony. "This is beautiful." The sun is dipping low, streaking the sky with soft pinks and oranges. Mist settles over the mountains in the distance.

Hunter joins me, wrapping his arms around my waist from behind. "I kind of miss this view. Miami is nice, but it's not this."

I glance back at him. "What's Miami like? Do you like it?"

"It's good," he says. "Hot. Busy. Loud. New." His grip tightens slightly. "But it feels incomplete without you."

I smile despite myself.

"If we're going to make this work, it's going to feel incomplete sometimes," I say gently. "At least for this year."

"I know." There's no hesitation in his voice. "You'll come down on breaks. I'll come up when I can. The possibilities are endless." He whispers it in my ear, like it's a secret.

I turn in his arms to face him, "I'd like that."

"Good." He says, kissing me softly before guiding me back inside. He closes the door behind me.

I hadn't noticed the champagne chilling on ice or the plate of chocolate-dipped strawberries waiting on the table. He grabs the bottle and pops the cork, pouring two glasses.

He lifts his toward me. "To you. Senior year. Make it a good one."

I raise mine. "And to you. First round. Kill it."

He laughs as our glasses clink. The bubbly drink tastes sweet and sharp on my tongue.

"I'm proud of you," I say again, quieter this time.

"I'm proud of you too," he replies easily.

I quirk a brow. "Me? Why?"

"Because, I know how hard it is for you to open up," he says softly. "To risk getting hurt. And you're doing it anyway. You're stepping outside your comfort zone for us. That matters."

I smile, thinking about how true that is. Before Hunter, I lived inside my little bubble. Safe. Predictable. It wasn't until he literally ran into me that everything shifted. I started saying yes more. Feeling more. Living more.

"You're worth it," I admit. "You sparked a light in me that had gone out. I don't know how else to explain it... but I'm glad you found me. What we have, is special... and I want to hold onto it."

His expression softens, then deepens. He set his glass aside and gently takes mine from my hand. The room feels smaller suddenly, warmer.

Before I can process what's happening, he lifts me effortlessly into his arms. I let out a small gasp, laughing as he carries me to the bed. He lays me down carefully, like I'm something precious. Then he reaches up and slides my glasses from my face, setting them aside.

I watch him through slightly blurred vision as he pulls his shirt over his head. He's broader than before. Stronger. The months of training evident in every line of him.

He unbuttons his jeans and slides them down his body, leaving only his clinging boxer briefs on him.

He removes my shoes first, slow and deliberate. My shorts follow. Then my shirt. Each touch intentional, unhurried. The moment his fingers touch my bare skin, my eyes flutter close as goosebumps rise. I've missed his touch so much. I'm already wet.

"You're so beautiful, Holly," he shakes his head as if in disbelief. "I've missed you. My soul aches without you."

My breath shudders. "I've missed you too."

His mouth claims mine again—deeper this time. Hungrier. Months of distance melting away in a single kiss.

The slow tenderness shifts, edged now with something rough, feral. Just how I like him; a little unhinged, a little greedy as he consumes my body. His hands are everywhere all at once. He unclasps my bra with ease, rips my undies completely off, licking on my neck and every inch of skin he can find. I don't even have time to think about it as he devours every inch of my body he can get. My body responds instantly, my hands and lips syncing with his moves. Every nerve on my body feels alive.

When he finally sinks fully into me, a moan so loud escapes my mouth that I'm suddenly grateful we're not back in my dorm room. It's been so long since I've felt him like this—skin to skin, heartbeat to heartbeat—and the sensation overwhelms me.

"God, you're so tight, baby," he breathes against my ear. My muscles convulse around him while he moves slowly, deliberately, drawing in and out at a measured pace, as if he's savoring every second. I feel everything—the heat of his skin, the rhythm of his breath, the quiet sounds he can't quite suppress. Our breaths tangle together, unsteady and intimate.

The room fades. The mountains. The city. The distance that once felt impossible. There's only us.

This man. He is everything. He is a part of my soul I refuse to let go.

And in this moment, wrapped around him, I know we'll be alright. I know we'll make it. Because he's right... we are endgame. And I'll be in his court. Forever.

CHAPTER 40

Hunter

Nine Months Later

With my first NBA season behind me, I finally feel at ease.

The game's slower now. The pressure more manageable. I signed a four-year contract with Miami—security I don't take for granted. More importantly, my health is much better. The team doctors have kept my HCM in check, and for the first time in years, I'm not playing with constant fear in the back of my mind.

Standing outside Hawks Arena, the memories hit hard.

College. March Madness. The grind. The beginning. My time here at Westbridge was a thrill.

Jalen approaches in his cap and gown, grinning wide.

"What up, Hunt? How's pro life treating you, big man?"

I clap his hand. "Can't complain. You declaring?"

He shrugs. "Maybe. If I'm lucky, I'd go second-round. If I get selected at all."

I pat him on his shoulder. "You got an invite, right?"

"Yeah."

"Then go," I tell him. "You've got nothing to lose."

He nods slowly. "Yeah. You're right." His gaze shifts past me. "You waiting on your girl?"

A grin spreads across my face before I can stop it. "Always."

"Tell Hols I said congrats," he says. "My family's over there."

"Will do, man. And hey, call me if you need anything. Pro advice, agents, whatever."

He bumps my shoulder and heads off. I turn back to the crowd, scanning for her. You'd think being six-nine would make this easy. But somehow, I still can't spot her.

The last nine months haven't been easy. Long distance never is. But we made it work. Late-night calls. Early-morning texts. Flights squeezed into off days. We chose each other every time.

And now she's graduated. In a couple weeks, she's moving to Miami, and already has a position lined up as an assistant literary agent—which, I know she's excited about. It still feels surreal.

It's a big leap for her. A new city. A new life. And I don't take it lightly.

I've got something planned tonight. Something she doesn't know about yet. And the anticipation is eating at me.

I finally see her. She's standing with a woman who looks just like her—her mom, I assume. Her dad's beside them, along with her brother and sister. I close the distance in a few strides.

"Hunter!" Holly lights up when she sees me. I'm holding flowers for her. She runs straight into my arms, and I lift her easily as she wraps herself around me. I kiss her softly.

"Hey, graduate," I murmur. "Congratulations."

She laughs, cupping my face. "Thanks."

I set her down as her family steps forward. Handshakes. Polite smiles. Quick hugs.

I spoke with her dad last month—a real conversation. An important one. It went well, thankfully. He seems like a solid guy.

After the ceremony, her family doesn't stay long. They've got a drive ahead of them. Holly and I walk back to her dorm, which is mostly packed up already. Some boxes went home with her parents earlier. The rest will be shipped down to Miami.

To our place.

She has a small overnight bag ready to go. I booked a room at the same Hilton I stayed at last summer. It feels fitting somehow.

And tonight, I'm finally ready to give the surprise I've been planning.

I grow more anxious as we reach the hotel and head toward the room. In the elevator, I adjust my suit for the dozenth time. The nerves are definitely kicking in now.

"Are you alright?' Holly asks, placing a hand on my arm.

"Yeah, I'm great." My voice pitches a little higher than usual.

"You sure?" she giggles.

Thankfully, the elevator dings before she can question me further. I take her hand and lead her down the hallway to the same room we stayed in last year.

I swipe the key and push the door open.

Red rose petals trail across the floor, leading into the room. Candles glow softly in glass jars, casting warm light along the walls.

Holly steps inside, her mouth falling open. "What is all this?" she whispers, taking everything in.

She looks stunning in her white graduation sundress. For a second, I have to steady myself, as I envision what's to hopefully come.

We follow the petals to the center of the room, where the candles form a circle. I drop to one knee.

"Hunter..." she gasps, hands flying to her mouth.

I swallow hard.

"From the moment we literally ran into each other, and I looked into your eyes, I knew you were different. You've had my attention from that second on. You're my peace, my strength, and the person who believes in me when I don't even believe in myself." My voice steadies as I look up at her. "You were never just a chapter to me. You're the whole story. Now and forever. Holly Lange, I love you more than anything. Will you marry me?"

Tears spill down her cheeks as I pull the small black velvet box and open it, revealing the two-carat oval solitaire ring inside. It was the first thing I bought with my NBA contract. And I've been waiting for this moment ever since.

She nods through her tears. "Yes, Hunt. Oh my God, yes!"

Relief crashes through me. I slide the ring onto her finger, stand, and pull her into my arms, lifting her off the ground as I kiss her.

I can't wait to start forever with my girl. My fiancée.

My endgame.

Acknowledgements

First of all, this book is dedicated to my time at Purdue University. The world of Westbridge State would not have come to life without it. I have such fond memories of my college days there, so to create a world inspired by it brought me a lot of joy and took me back to the fun and thrill of my college experience.

I want to of course thank my husband for being incredibly supportive of my writing journey and allowing me the space to do so while taking care of our three little boys, who are nothing but chaos. Thank you to my dearest friend, Jacquie B. for always being there to bounce ideas back and forth and to help with cover tweaks. Your friendship is a true blessing in my life.

Thank you to my editor, Kriti, for helping make my stories shine. Thank you to Rachel at MeetCuteMarketing for managing ARCs and being super supportive when things are going a bit haywire. Thank you to my BETA and ARC readers, especially those that got back to me with manuscript errors. I can't tell you how much I appreciate your eagle eyes!!

I also want to express my greatest thanks to Mary, thesleepingfoxy, for the gorgeous character artwork that graces the cover.

Lastly, thank you to all my readers and supporters. Thank you for going on these incredible stories with me!

The Westbridge State Series

Interested in diving back into the world of Westbridge State?
Next up is Brandy and Nash's story.
Coming in 2027

character illustration by thesleepingfoxy

For more updates and bonus content, sign up for my newsletter at http://amandacirilliauthor.com

ABOUT THE AUTHOR

Author Photography by Kristen Trent photography

Amanda Cirilli is a romance author who writes characters with high emotional stakes and the obstacles they must overcome to receive their happy ending.

Amanda lives in North Georgia with her husband and is a mom to three amazing little boys, and a dog. When she has some spare time, she loves reading and writing, of course, as well as watching true crime documentaries/shows, Netflix, and her favorite sports teams. She is also a lover of Disney and Spongebob Squarepants. Amanda also loves performing with community theater companies (if she ever has time).

OTHER WORKS:
The Starlight Princess

FOR MORE INFORMATION VISIT:
http://amandacirilliauthor.com

OR FOLLOW ON SOCIAL MEDIA:
@amanda.cirilli.author
TikTok
Instagram
Threads
Facebook

www.ingramcontent.com/pod-product-compliance
Lightning Source LLC
LaVergne TN
LVHW041146150826
845673LV00001B/80

* 9 7 9 8 9 9 9 7 4 5 8 4 2 *